Peace River Country

Peace River Country

Ralph Allen

Doubleday & Company, Inc.

Garden City, New York

All of the characters in this book are fictitious,
and any resemblance to actual persons, living or dead,
is purely coincidental.

Peace River Country

Chapter One

To Harold, shrunk tautly into the backward-riding side of the double seat, their going away—like their coming—was a flight. No matter how much Kathleen and their mother tried to make it seem like something else, he was not going to help the pretense or to enter into it. They were running away and in this there was nothing good or hopeful, although he did see its necessity.

Kally was full of oafish, unreckoning excitement. She was kneeling on the other side of the seat, blowing furiously on the window, then blowing on her woolen mitts and rubbing a widening porthole in the window's thick coat of frost. Occasionally she stopped rubbing, to press her nose against the window and shout back an inventory of the contents of the dark station platform outside.

"There goes Mr. Groton!" she shouted. "Three bags of mail. And one *huge* parcel, it looks like Eaton's. I'll bet it's the new septic tank for Dr. Finlayson."

Harold appealed to their mother with a glance of indignation. But Mrs. Sondern seemed not to have heard. She was standing in the aisle of the ancient day coach, with one hand resting on the top of the upended wicker suitcase and the other pressed hard against the scratchy maroon top of the double seat, almost as though she and the two objects were a chain and if she let go of either the suitcase or the railway coach, they would fly apart and leave her empty-handed.

"Mother," Harold said anxiously, "have you got the tickets?"

"What? Oh yes, of course I've got them, Harold."

"There's Barb and Lucy," Kally shouted. The shout mounted to a shriek. "Good-by, Barb! 'By, Lucy. Barb!" She quieted and gave the window another matter-of-fact rub. "They didn't hear me," she reported. There was neither disappointment nor humility in her voice and in a moment it rose again.

"Hi, Barb! Hi, Lucy!" She lowered her tone to an excited piercing whisper. "They see me now." She pounded insanely at the window and put her face back to it and yelled: "When we get to where we're going I'll send you my address and you can write."

She didn't even add "if you like," Harold noted with a shudder. He glanced anxiously down the aisle of the railway car. He saw with relief that the car had only one other occupant, probably a city man, dozing.

"Make her stop that awful noise," Harold hissed.

"She's just saying good-by." Mrs. Sondern gave him an affectionate now-now-Harold smile.

"In a minute she'll be babbling where we're going and then the first thing anybody knows . . ." He did not complete the sentence.

Their mother, only a little plumper and a little less pretty than Kally and a shade less idiotically shining, turned her head away for an instant. She was smiling when she looked at him again. She stood up, removed her gray woolen mittens, squirmed out of the lightly mottled maroon overcoat that had obviously been dyed, cut down, and once a man's, and finally eased a knitted green-and-orange toque off her head in a careful, front-to-back motion like the last brushing of a pompadour. Except for a very minor wisp of gray sitting lightly on each bulbous ear bun, her hair was as dark and thick as Kally's and her cheeks, as they always were in winter, were of the lacquer-smooth redness which is just a few seconds short of frostbite.

She sat down, smoothed her stringy wine-colored knitted suit, and reached across to pat Harold's hand. "Don't worry!" she said gently.

The train sighed and humped into motion, its tracks shrieking desolately in the snow.

"We're going!" Kally yelled. "Good-by, Dobie!"

Mrs. Sondern leaned across Kally's hunched shoulder and whispered softly through the frost-freed porthole at the lonely squares of light in the freight-shed window: "Good-by, Dobie."

Kally was chanting the old school yell.

> "Dobie Dobie Osky-Zops
> Dobie Hit 'Em in the Chops.
> Dobie. Dobie. Dob-ee-ee."

"Aren't you going to say good-by to Dobie, Harold?" Mrs. Sondern asked quietly when Kally fell silent.

"I think that gentleman is trying to sleep," Harold mumbled.

The round mountainous shadows of the water tower and the grain elevator glided past and then they were plunging recklessly into the black empty prairie, unprepared for their coming by the measure of a single gleam of starlight. The gaslit day coach was full of hostile smells: chipped varnish blended with worn plush and used dust, and outside the quietly rattling doorway the cold steam couplings hissed and clanked like the sound of a duel between dragons and men in armor.

Harold looked at the other two, half daring them now to sustain their foolish gaiety and half afraid that they would not.

"It's a fine little town," Mrs. Sondern said gravely. "Such fine, friendly neighbors. Not the same opportunities there, of course."

Kally sat forward eagerly. "Have you decided what we'll do when we get to the Pea——"

"Mother!" Harold had made up his mind that the city man couldn't possibly be asleep. "Make her stop blabbing everything. The first thing anybody knows . . ." Again he could not find words to finish the bitter thought.

"It's all right, dear," Mrs. Sondern said sympathetically. "It doesn't really matter if anybody knows."

Kally said without rancor: "What have you decided we'll do when we get there?"

"Well, now——" In spite of himself Harold could not altogether divorce himself from the buoyancy of his mother's undertone. "—I meant to tell you today but in all the hurry and excitement I forgot. Mrs. Barbour was in Winnipeg last week and she says needlepoint's all the rage. I might just try that for a while."

"Needlepoint!" Kally gasped. "Why, Mother, that's an inspiration."

"They sell a little piece hardly bigger than a handkerchief for as much as twenty dollars," Mrs. Sondern said. She added in a less confident tone, for Harold: "Of course it's very difficult."

"Just think!" Kally glowed. "Twenty dollars for a piece hardly as big as a handkerchief. Why, you could make fifty or sixty dollars a month easily—poof! more like a hundred dollars when you get the hang of it."

Harold did not wish to be enticed into the discussion. He didn't really want to withdraw from this particular hope until a likelier one offered itself, but on the other hand he did not want to subscribe to it and he felt that in letting it go unchallenged he would be deemed to have subscribed.

"Gosh, Mother," he said, "isn't needlepoint that fancy sewing stuff? What would they want to buy it up there for?"

"That's just it!" Kally cut in. "They can't get things like that up there."

"But half of it's unbroken country"—Harold looked straight across the seat at his mother, trying to ignore Kally's immature interruptions—"I heard you say that lots of the women up there still do the stooking and help out with the hay."

"That's just it, silly," Kally broke in again. The tender triumphant glance she bestowed first on Harold and then on their mother invited her to join in friendly toleration of his innocence. "That's just it. They've got lots of money. But no nice things. Nice things are just what a lady wants in a place like that."

"You never can be sure about things like that, Harold," Mrs. Sondern said gently. "You never can be sure until you try. Now let's all try to get a little sleep."

Harold closed his eyes, trying to shut out the light from the prehistoric gas lamp above his head. But he only suc-ceeded in trapping the light and shutting it in, and the more tightly he squeezed his eyelids, the brighter the light be-came. Across this plane of light a chain of visions raced, sometimes just under its glaring green surface and sometimes just above it, like crazed sea-things chasing each other through a phosphorescent swell. He couldn't catch any one thing and hold it long enough for study. One moment there was a shape as clear and unforgettable as the face of his fa-ther, seen less than half an hour ago. But in the next moment the whitely drooping mask of flesh dissolved completely and in its place there was an image he could only identify by the name of Going. Going was not a new image, but it was a harder one to keep hold of, for it was without corporate limits, a black undulation of mass without form. And then there was Money—not altogether separate from Going and therefore not altogether unlike it, but with many daylight things floating in and out of comprehension on its own dark wave, the laundry wagon, for instance, and his mother's thin, scuffed black change purse. At last, as he had hoped desperately that it would, the new place, the place where they were going, swept into the center of his ken. For a moment it hung there all alone, green and quiet, but it would not stay. His father's face began to return and he opened his eyes.

In the seat across from him Kally was already fast asleep in the yellow light, her head cradled above her bundled winter reefer on the swaying window sill. Their mother sat beside her, awake.

"Come over here," Harold whispered.

His mother smiled as she drew his head close. Harold looked down the car again. The city man was snoring softly.

"Let's talk about the Peace River Country," he whispered.

"We're going to love it, Harold. It's a very big and splendid place. Everybody says that."

"Yes," he said, demanding to be mollified. "But not the way Kally thinks."

"Perhaps not." She paused, thinking hard. "But perhaps so."

"Mother," Harold said abruptly, sitting forward so that he could look straight into her face, "did you think Dobie was a good place? Really?"

Her sure, quiet expression did not waver. "Why, yes, Harold. Didn't you?"

"I don't know," he said miserably. "What about Regina?"

"Yes, I always liked Regina."

"Then why didn't we stay?" The image of his father leaped at him from the yellow gaslight hanging overhead and he shrank back against his mother's breast to take refuge from his own despicableness. "I mean, if we could have," he blurted. "I mean, is the place we're going so much *better?*"

"Oh yes, Harold," she whispered. "Yes. Yes. Dobie and Regina are good places, but they're not *famous* for being good. They're not famous all over the world."

"I never heard you say much about it before today." Now he wished above everything else to share her intensity and enthusiasm and he said the words in such a way as to make it clear that he was merely pointing to a curious deficiency in his background.

"That's only because it's so far away."

"How long will it take to get there?" Again he was careful that no hint of skepticism or unease should enter his voice.

"Oh, goodness." His mother's tone indicated it was a triviality but an interesting enough triviality over which to pass the time. "Perhaps a month. Perhaps two."

"Gee, that's not so long, is it?"

"Back in '32, or perhaps '31—the drought was even worse then, or it *seemed* worse because it was so much newer; that was quite a while before we came to Dobie—well, a few years back—one family went all the way up there with a team of horses and a wagon."

"Two thousand miles with one team and wagon!"

"It took them nearly two years. But they wrote back that it was worth every bit of it. Every bit of it and more. They wrote back that they never have droughts there, or grasshoppers or rust or anything like that. And the land is cheap. In some parts they can still get homesteads. The strangest thing, the thing nobody could believe when the country was opened up, is the climate. Even away up north like that the weather is away better than the weather here. It's the chinooks."

"I don't think the chinooks go up that far, do they?" Harold was offering light conversation, rather than an argument.

"Then it must be the monsoons. It's a much better climate anyway."

"It's a pretty big country, isn't it?" The talk was rolling beautifully now.

"Absolutely huge. Right from here, right from Dobie and Carsdale and Collington, just from this one little corner of Saskatchewan, nearly fifty families went up there in the bad times. Counting the people from other places there were thousands and thousands of people that went and there was room for everybody and there's still room for lots more. Why, it's so big it's in two provinces. It starts in Alberta and goes right over into B.C."

"How come you know so much about it, Mother?" Harold mumbled lazily.

"Oh, I've been thinking about it for years. Your father and I always wanted——" She paused, and went on quickly. "—I used to read about it a lot. I used to get out a map and look at all the towns and try and see which one I'd pick out if I ever went there."

"What one will we go to?"

"I always thought Grande Prairie. That's the biggest town."

"It's a nice name."

"Names! If you want names! You never heard such names. The first people that went up there saw it was a different kind of country and when they started picking the names . . ."

"What are some of them?" he asked, suddenly almost eager.

"Oh, let me see. I don't suppose I'll be able to remember all of them. Well, just to take some of the other Prairies, there's a Rose Prairie, and a High Prairie and a Clear Prairie."

"Mmuh?"

"Oh and there's a Progress and even a Rio Grande. And

a Valhalla and I think, yes, I'm sure, there's a Bonanza."

"Gee, and down here the best names they can think of are names like Dobie and Oxbow and Carnduff."

"There's a Heart Valley too, Harold. I don't know why I didn't think of it before. It was always my favorite. There's a Lone Star and a Sunrise Valley."

"Any more?" he murmured.

"There's a Cherry Hill."

"Cherry Hill!"

"Oh, and a Blueberry Mountain."

Harold thought briefly of asking whether anybody who was trying to find a person up there would have trouble finding them if the person didn't want to be found. He now believed the question to be unnecessary.

He yawned happily and then said importantly: "When we get to Elevator I'll get a job. In a place that big I'll bet they need all kinds of delivery boys and things. I'll get a job and then we'll be able to get moving again just that much faster."

She gave him a gentle hug. "We'll see about that. Anyway, we always make out somehow, don't we?"

"Sure we do," he said staunchly. He squeezed her soft hand and in a moment he was sleeping, placidly and undreaming.

Chapter Two

"Elevator." The brakeman had been through earlier and turned down all the lights except the one at the far end of the car. The conductor's face was ghostly, like the voice he had solicitously lowered for the benefit of the sleeping children. "Elevator," the conductor said again, reaching across and removing the ticket stubs from behind the metal catch of the window blind.

It was not an outright question, but it was plain that the conductor would be disappointed if he did not receive an answer.

"We have friends there," Mrs. Sondern said.

"Oh yes."

She perceived at once that she had said a silly thing. This must be the Mr. Chatsworth who had been traveling up and down the line so long that he was known as CPR Chatsworth in every one of its twenty-odd villages and hamlets and in the two full-fledged towns at its terminals. "I'm Mrs. Sondern," she said quickly, as though to forestall an accusation. She could think of no way to retrieve the untruth about the friends in Elevator and yet so long as it lay between them, she recognized that it might be difficult for him not to feel sorry for her.

"Of course," she said, prompted by a small inspiration, "we probably won't *stay* with them. I imagine we'll stay at the hotel. I hear it's very comfortable."

"Yes," the conductor said sadly.

"We're really only stopping over long enough to do some shopping," she plunged on firmly, hoping that he would go away.

"Yes." His sorrow for them had become almost unbearable.

She went on, comforting him. "We're actually going to the Peace River Country."

He stifled a sigh. "I used to know your husband," he said.

"He's coming on later," she said. "He's staying in Dobie for a few days"—the phrase settled snugly into place—"winding up our affairs."

"Yes."

It was an effort not to reach out and pat the kind, melancholy man on the arm. "Well," he groaned, "I'm sure they'll miss you folks in Dobie."

"We'll miss Dobie too," she said. She meant it thoroughly. She had never known anything but happiness there.

There had been, perhaps, a feeling of uneasiness between them and the village. But never more than that. They had moved there when Kally was going on six and Harold was going on seven, the day after New Year's, 1933, the day after she had decided that they must leave Regina.

Mr. Sondern had once clerked in the bank in Dobie and during the last few years he had often spoken of the village with a befuddled repining not unnatural to his natural state. Mrs. Sondern couldn't think of a better place to move to.

Mr. Sondern had made no great impact there himself, but when the story got back to the village, as it inevitably did in spite of his wife's staunch evasions, that he had become one of Regina's most indefatigable alcoholics, the village began to utter his name with a certain reverence. A village drunk is an object of pity or ridicule; but a city drunk, a man who is such a spectacular drunk that a provincial capital concedes his fame and his entitlement to be exclaimed over and deplored—this latter drunk, this city drunk, acquires something near to majesty. Although it was agreed in Dobie that Chris Sondern had done a disreputable thing, there was also something large and exotic about it. In time his memory achieved a minor canonization. "Poor Sondern, he was a brilliant man," the bank manager, Mr. Dobbs, used to say, with more respect for dramatic effect than for the demonstrable facts. The legend that Chris Sondern might have been a great man if only he hadn't taken to drink germinated and took root, and this gave his family the complicated problem of both living up to his memory and living it down when they went back to live among his old neighbors.

They had been, at any rate, legitimate objects of curiosity. Occasionally Mrs. Sondern conceded secretly that they might be causing embarrassment to the village. She fully understood that it might have been embarrassing the way they moved at first into a cottage by the river and insisted on staying there until the first blizzards came and froze them out. She fully understood that she might have caused embarrassment, after they moved into the town house, through her insistence on paying rent every month, particularly during those months when the first of the month arrived and she didn't have the rent. But she had the children's feelings to consider first, and on the whole she couldn't have asked for better neighbors.

She knew in her heart of hearts that she was not good at doing laundry and from the first she had clear inner intimations that her laundry service tyrannized and disrupted the village in a rather regrettable degree. Not that she ever did less than her best. For the first year she was there, almost everybody who sent washing out sent it to her, and she attacked each wash with happy, optimistic ferocity, hurling socks, towels, table linen and colored shirts and dresses into a foaming bath of suds and then beating the whole mixture into a pulpy mash with a broomstick handle. Little evil-smelling blobs of wool floated through it and became imbedded in the fabric of unaffiliated underclothing. Colors ran and realigned themselves in sensationally incompatible combinations. Woolen socks shrank and hardened vilely, and lesser fabrics slowly disintegrated under the assault of strong lye soap and physical violence. Sometimes, late at night, when the children were asleep, she found herself in tears for her customers' underthings and for the beauty of spirit which prompted them to suffer, and suffer again, without reproach.

In time she improved. But she was not in the least surprised by the lack of public consternation which greeted her announcement that she wouldn't have time to do any more laundry. Harold was fond of answering advertisements, and it was an advertisement for a home knitting machine that induced her to abandon her laundry clients.

She obtained the knitting machine on credit. According to the literature of the company which sold it to her, the profits would pay for it within three months and leave her a minimum profit of seven dollars a week for the rest of the foreseeable future. Kally amended this figure sharply upward. "If we all pitch in, we can keep the machine going all day instead of the few easy hours a week they talk about." Even Harold put more stock in the knitting machine than he had put in the washing and was sufficiently encouraged to speak of a Mickey Cochrane catcher's mitt for his birthday. Kally planned a new suit for Easter.

Mrs. Sondern assaulted the knitting machine with the same gallant savagery she had brought to bear on the washtub. Although it had been represented to her in the directions that the knitting of socks by machine was a simple mathematical process, the socks which Mrs. Sondern knitted were a challenge and an affront to mathematics. They had no visible connection with mathematics at all. There was no rote or consistency to them; they emerged from the machine with staggering qualities of individualness, some shaped like crescents, some like thumbless mittens, some like square lengths of stovepipe, some lean and close-grained in texture, some obese and tired, some unkempt and tufted, like the morning hair of small mole-colored boys. However, she had followed the directions very carefully and she assured herself that there could be nothing fundamentally wrong.

Before she shipped away the first half dozen sets of two she conferred briefly with the children.

"They don't seem to be all the same size," Harold suggested. At this time Harold was eight and, although fiercely loyal, he had begun to develop a nervous streak of practicalness.

"Of course they're not all the same size," Kally sniffed. "You suppose all *feet* are the same size?"

Mrs. Sondern's confidence rallied. She smiled wisely. "Machine socks never look right until they're washed," she told Harold.

"You gonna wash them before you send them?" Harold asked hopefully.

"No," Mrs. Sondern said. She added, "The instructions don't say to wash them. I think they've got some special kind of machine at the factory. It makes them come out nicer."

There followed three weeks of waiting. An exciting cloud-head of suspense built up above the town house—all the more exciting because, by tacit understanding, its existence was denied formal recognition. The admission of suspense would have been an admission of doubt. Kally and her mother were too proud to doubt and even Harold seemed to realize doubt was now a dangerous luxury.

The socks were never mentioned by name. The gaunt, Goldbergish knitting machine, temporarily without wool to feed it, was retired to a remote corner of the living-room table. Such references as it was found necessary to make about the waiting were carefully oblique.

"Any mail tonight?" Mrs. Sondern would manage a stifled yawn when Kally or Harold, whosever turn it was, came back from meeting the train from the East.

"Only one bag for the whole town."

"I kind of thought Aunt Virgie might be writing."

And then, abruptly and insultingly, the socks were there again, dispersed across the foothills of the sway-backed living-room table amid a thicket of hurriedly torn wrapping paper and string, a gray unwanted effluvium.

"Regret . . . do not meet our specifications." Mrs. Sondern read the letter with rising indignation.

Kally's voice was shrill. "They're just trying to get out of paying!"

She picked up one of the socks. "Look!" she said triumphantly. "They never even put it through the washing machine. It's just the same as it was before."

"That proves it!" Harold spoke with less conviction, but he was in the spirit of it. "That proves it. They're just trying to get out of paying."

They sat for a while in an odd strained silence, alternately inspecting the rejected socks and the letter, each taking a secret satisfaction from the world's corruption and each balancing this satisfaction against a secret melancholy. Their sense of outrage and injustice, at first so sure and exhilarating, suddenly went sodden and shapeless, like the worst of the socks themselves. Curiously enough it was Harold, the least resilient normally, who was the first to react. He began to hum one of their finest hymns, softly and absently, as though the impulse were subconscious.

Then they were all singing, robustly and splendidly, not singing for religion but, as they always did, for recreation, not singing to any identifiable God but singing to each other.

> "When the roll . . .
> "When the roll . . .
> "When the roll is called up yonder,
> "When the roll is called up yonder,
> "I'll be there."

They sang the hymn over several times, and then they sang "Jesus Lover," "What A Friend," "Rock of Ages," and half a dozen others. In the final silence Mrs. Sondern panted glowingly. "Well! Singing always tuckers me right out. I think I'll go and make us all a nice cup of cocoa."

A little later she called from the kitchen: "Clear a place, will you, Harold?"

Harold shoved his stuff a little way down one of the warped slopes of the table and rearranged Kally's crayons in an adjoining valley. Then, without really looking at it, as though this were only an afterthought, he picked up the knitting machine and took it into the bedroom. Mrs. Sondern heard a muffled scraping as he made gangway for it in the back of the clothes closet. They never spoke of it again.

Mr. Chatsworth's hand, plucking at her arm, was as gentle and far away as the rhythm of the train.

"Would you like some hot cocoa?" His sad, heavy face was florid under the streaks of dawn. She blinked from him to the faces of the sleeping children. "I mean, would you all like some cocoa?" he asked.

"It's very good of you." She shivered drowsily.

"We have a caboose on tonight," he said quickly. "It will

just go to waste. There are a few sandwiches too and I thought the children . . ."

"What time will we be in?" she asked uncertainly. "I wouldn't want to spoil their breakfast."

"About fifty minutes."

"Well, then, thank you very much, but . . ." Then she remembered that she had gone to sleep thinking about breakfast for the children. She was anticipating no difficulty about it, really; still—"Well, if you're *sure* it won't be used."

"I'll bring it up here," he said, and lumbered off down the aisle.

Mrs. Sondern sat up and rotated her neck, then leaned back against the dusty plush back of the seat, studying the thin sunrise at rest on the faces of the children.

She had meant to have a lot of children, and it was remarkable that she had managed to stop at two. Harold was born at the end of the first year of her marriage. Kathleen was born thirteen months later, when Mr. Sondern was entering his second year of sickness.

Mrs. Sondern had decided she hadn't better have any more children until her husband felt better. She never referred to his condition, or often thought of it, in terms more pessimistic than these, but just the same she stopped having children.

It was a hard thing for her to do. She had a strong instinct for motherhood, and she bore children easily. For all except a few slate-gray minutes she had been fully conscious each time; and when the midwife—the Regina doctors were asking twenty-five dollars a confinement—had said, for Harold, "It's a boy," and, for Kally, "A girl," Mrs. Sondern had been able to speak out the name, clear and strong.

The bedroom was a narrow shoe box above a boarding-house garage, but there was a window on each side with a Manitoba maple chinning itself on the lower sill. In the instant that she first saw each of her children, she also saw the sky—sunset for Harold, sunrise for Kally, a fine fall day for each, with the summer dust storms past and the snow not yet arrived.

Long afterward, when the children were out playing or meeting the train, she sat alone in the house in Dobie beside the west window, watching the sun go down and keeping tryst with the ghosts of other Harolds. More rarely, long before anyone else was up, she would start to wakefulness at dawn—suddenly, as though roused by a muffled cry—pull her decayed kimono around her goose-pimpled shoulders, slip past Harold's bed in the front room and stand barefooted at the little square of glass in the kitchen door, looking silently across the roof of the cowshed to where the first color of morning spilled upward on the heaped leftover clouds of the night before. Then she would think of other Kallys.

Sunset for Harold, sunrise for Kally. The thought was mysterious and thrilling and, of course, a little sad. Sometimes, reflecting in this vein, she felt that she was reliving the distant physical adventures over again, down to their most elusive and debatable details; the small, symbolic rustling she still thought she'd seen among the maple trees just before the door whispered open from the kitchen and she turned her eyes from the window to look toward the woman; the ticking of the alarm clock on the dresser, sounding louder than it had for some hours, and more relieved; the thin smell of steam, unreasonably self-assertive above the pungency of antiseptics; and finally the first timid feel of her fingers on new flesh, her flesh . . . yes, God's flesh, so soft and tender that she shuddered with the sacred wonder of it.

Remembering this way, it was always an effort to shut out the other part. Depending on whether it was morning or night, she would turn away from the window right in the middle of the memory and hurry to the stove to light the fire or drive herself stoically back to the unfinished ironing on the living-room table. But the other part always intruded, the part that said solemnly: *Two aren't enough. They'll grow up. Two aren't enough. They'll grow up and leave you.*

These eddies of terror were never more than eddies. It was never very long before she was able to lose them in the reassuring luxury of finding Kally's other stocking for her, or of coaxing Harold to take his cascara. And, of course, in the more rational hours between dawn and dusk their falsity couldn't even stand up against ordinary logic.

Mrs. Sondern would have been the last to say, as she often said, that her children were any different than anybody else's. But surely, leaving every distinction of human quality out of it, it was still apparent that the more dependent people were on each other to begin with, the more dependent on each other they must always remain. When you had sense enough to be logical about it, the very size of their family—three—had special and demonstrable properties of unity. If you were more than three, you spread out too much, nothing could be shared perfectly, there were too many experiences that someone would miss through the laws of chance alone. And if you were only two, there was only the one bond; no matter how strong it was, there was no other, and if it weakened everything weakened. But with three, there were three bonds, all reinforcing each other and drawing in the same direction.

Sunset for Harold, sunrise for Kally. But what for Chris? For him time needed another shape, faceless, indistinct, withholding. Why Chris, the most needful, more needful even than Harold, who had been the one that had to be shut out? Why the lover cut off from love, the father exiled from fatherhood?

The train plunged through the winter morning and for the woman gazing out the window each swift cold click its wheels made against the separations in the rails was a cry of protest. *Bea! Bea! Bea!* The wheels called her name with the stifled, frozen urgency of a voice crying into darkness.

"I should have left him a note," she said, half aloud. "Not to tell him where we're going, not to say anything that would make him feel worse. I just should have left him a note to say where he could find things. Things to eat and that."

Bea! Bea! Bea! the wheels called to her. Yes, Chris, I hear. I've always heard. Always, always heard.

It could not be otherwise. It would not ever be. He was a part of everything here—of the perky, radiant half-belligerent look on Kally's sleeping face, of the dark, sober *thinking* set to Harold's tightened mouth.

Chris had a part in the mystery and excitement of this night on the moving train. Whether it was as exalted as lying still in bed or as homely as sprinkling brown sugar over a bowl of porridge, or as anxious as counting up the money for the rent, the spectrum of living held no shade whose study had not been shared with him. When you married you did not just marry a person, you married a universe, a whole new set of meanings.

Even God changed. In His own good time, God would reunite her with the dark, unfathomed man she had sworn and never ceased to love and honor; any other thought was unbearable. You had to keep this ultimate hope at all costs, but in the meantime it was necessary to recast the old ideas of a God who distributed justice and mercy with an easy unfailing generosity. You had to be prepared to hoe a long and complicated row; depending on hope as much as you could, but not too much, in your passing day-to-day affairs.

Counting on things too much was never safe. But counting too little was just as bad. Once, long before their parting, she had thought Chris was gone forever. She had been very sick, with a disease really meant for children, scarlet fever. Kally had had it first and just at the end of nursing her through, Bea herself had had to go to bed, delirious and chased by shadows of guilt and disaster. While she was sick-

est Chris had stayed near. Each night he sat beside her on
a wooden chair and held her hand, sipping only as often as
he had to from a bottle of loganberry wine. Each morning
he phoned the place where he held a bad job by a slender
thread and told a new lie or elaborated on an old lie about
why he would not be able to come to work. He had lost the
right to tell the truth, alas. He had already called so often
to mumble that his wife was ill, or had Bea call to say that
he was ill, that when illness really was upon them there was
nothing left but to say there had been a fire in the basement.
He kept explaining that immense, half-specified complica-
tions concerning plumbing, heating, sanitation and public
safety forced him to remain at home and wait upon the in-
spectors. It was fairly well understood, of course, that Chris's
superior did not believe any of this. But there was enough
novelty behind it so that he did not have to feel his intelligence was being insulted. The people at the office pretended to accept Chris's excuses during the three worst days
of Bea's illness. On the fourth day they told him not to come
back at all.

Bea was much better by then. She was sitting up and
Aunt Virgie had been able to come over for a day or two
to help with the children's meals. Chris came into the bedroom and put his hand on Bea's forehead.

"You're cool and sweet as could be," he said.

"I feel fine." Bea reached up and squeezed his slender
hand.

"I think I'll go out for a while," Chris said to her.

"It's time you got some fresh air," Bea answered softly.
She was not sure that she would ever see him again. But
she was not clever enough to know a better way of express-
ing all the wispy unfinished thoughts that drift above the
no man's land of love, thickening and suddenly vanishing
like the tag ends of a fog. "It's time you got some fresh air."

"Well, then——"

It did not pay to give up on hope. Two days afterward Chris came back. He was pale and bearded and nearly spent. In one hand he held out a quart bottle of chocolate milk, a rare thing in those earlier times.

"I thought I'd get you this," he said. "You could have some and so could the children."

"We'll all like it so much," Bea answered.

"What is it, Mother?" Harold's dark eyes had opened and he was studying her face with uneasy concern. "What are you worrying about?"

"Worrying, dear? Oh, I wasn't exactly worrying. I was just doing some mental arithmetic. You know, if it takes on, I believe the needlepoint will be an even better thing than we've been figuring."

The door at the end of the coach belched open and the conductor swept down the aisle behind a gust of fresh morning air.

"Here it is." He placed a tin tray of sandwiches and mugs filled with cocoa on the seat beside Kally. Then he hurried away again. Mrs. Sondern shook the girl quietly but insistently to wakefulness.

"First call for breakfast," she said with an unobtrusive gaiety suitable to the hour. "Next stop Elevator, Sask. All change."

Chapter Three

If it had been anyone else at the door, Lonnie Rivers would not have opened at that hour of the morning. A village bootlegger, like a village doctor or a village lawyer, had certain responsibilities to his community. The responsibility of seeing that no one was permitted to buy a drink before sundown, except on Saturdays, was one of these.

Now, as he looked through the tiny square of glass in the pounding storm door, Lonnie Rivers saw that it was barely dawn. After a moment he recognized the face on the other side as the face of Chris Sondern and he acted on a higher responsibility and opened the door. It was to be expected that Chris Sondern would call around. It was to be expected that he would require a drink and that after he had had a drink or two he would throw enlightenment on the tumultuous mysteries of the last sixteen hours. It was to be expected that any public-spirited citizen of Dobie would welcome this enlightenment, rather than repel it, and see that it received its proper place in the history of the town.

He opened the door.

"Hello"—he hesitated very briefly over the form of address—"Mr. Sondern. If I hadn't heard you was in town I wouldn't have known it was you." He spoke the truth. Sondern was much thinner and older than he had been thirteen years before, but the dimensions of time and physical change were not fully adequate to describe what had happened to him. He looked as shrunk and beat-up as a stillborn calf. Lonnie held the phrase in his mind, not precisely with pleasure and certainly not with malice, but confident that it would serve well later. Sondern's face was pinched with cold and thirst and his eyes were so watery with the cold that when he reached up to dry them the water sloshed off the back of his thin white hand and made a dark patch of wet the size of a small saucer on the sleeve of his overcoat. The coat itself was both grotesquely large and grotesquely insufficient, one of those frail dark, genteel velvet-collared garments that were seen in their days of full splendor only on the very rich, and in their days of ultimate decay only on the very poor. With the coat he was wearing a worn gray tweed cap with one ear flap down and the other apparently wasted away, leaving a gap of space between a part of the cap and a part of his head. When he saw Lonnie staring at the cap he took it off, put it on a chair beside the kitchen table, and pushed the chair out of sight beneath the table. The gesture was unconscious, but it was a gesture. It seemed to remind him that he had the power of movement. He walked with surprising briskness around the table, stamped his feet loudly, and sat down in a chair on the other side.

"How's it going, Lonnie?" he asked in an astonishingly quiet and ordinary voice. He did not wait for an answer, however, or act as though he expected one. He reached quickly into the breast pocket of his overcoat and extracted two carefully wadded two-dollar bills with the air of a man who always knows exactly how much money he has and what pocket it's in. He laid them on the table challengingly, as though grown accustomed to a minimum of attention until his money had been produced and examined.

"You don't need to do that," Lonnie Rivers said.

"Catawba."

"I don't sell it. I sometimes keep a little extra for my friends." Lonnie made the demurrer through force of habit as he moved toward the open pantry at the end of the bare, dawn-lit kitchen.

Sondern sipped the first glass slowly, fondling rather than gulping the dark native wine, but holding the glass at the level of his lips, never more than an inch away until it was empty. His hand was surprisingly steady as he refilled it from the quart bottle Lonnie had placed on the linoleum-topped table.

"Mind if I take off my coat?"

"Well, gotta get to work pretty soon."

"You still at the livery stable?"

"Uh-huh. I don't know why he keeps it up any more. Maybe one team a day. Three—four on Saturday. That's in winter."

Sondern took off his overcoat, shrugging its armpits across the back of his chair. His blue suit was dirty and creased, but it was a reasonable fit. The removal of the overcoat presented him for the first time in a manageable medium of comparison. He still looked shrunk and beat-up, but not grotesquely so, not much more so than other men Lonnie had seen going on for forty, for baldness, and out of the last hangover into the next.

"Say," Lonnie said, "*you* ain't changed so much."

Sondern poured his third glass of wine and drank it down. "Who said I had?"

"Funny how many people's left since you did. Dobbs, he retired. Gone to Vancouver Island. Up the coast some place. Man named Ellis got the bank now."

"Who said I had?"

"Said what?"

"Changed?"

"I donno, Chris."

"I guess we better have another bottle." Lonnie went to the pantry.

Sondern drank again.

"How did you know I was in town?" Lonnie couldn't tell how the wine was sitting on him. He spoke slowly, but quite clearly.

"Oh, I donno. Somebody was saying up at the post office last night."

"I'll bet they were saying plenty up at the post office last night." Sondern subsided into a gloomy petulant silence. After a while he sprang excitedly to his feet and said eagerly: "Got a pack of cards?"

"What——?"

"Come on, let's have the cards. Let's have them."

Lonnie went to the pantry and came back with a limp handful of blue-backed Bicycles. "There's only forty-eight or forty-nine," he said.

"Doesn't matter." Sondern took the cards and shuffled them with clumsy haste. Two or three fell between his excited fingers to the floor. "Doesn't matter a bit," he said. He offered the pack face down to the other man. "Take any one," he said. "Go on, any one at all."

Lonnie took a card from the middle of the pack and stole an uncomfortable look at it.

"Now put it back."

Sondern shuffled the cards, holding their faces away from him at arm's length and squeezing his dark eyes tightly and ostentatiously shut.

"Now," he said, "now we'll see." He opened his eyes and ran eagerly through the cards. He held up the five of hearts.

"That it?"

"That's her."

"You damn right that's her!" Sondern rasped grandly. "Try another."

He repeated the performance several times. Then he handed the pack to Rivers. "You try it," he commanded defiantly.

Rivers backed away from the proffered deck. "Hell, I couldn't do it," he mumbled.

"Well, try it. Try it anyway."

"No, I couldn't."

Sondern threw the cards carelessly to the linoleum-topped table. "You damn right you couldn't do it!" he said exultantly. "Nobody in this whole town could do it."

He sat down and refilled his glass. "Not a one of them could do it. Lousy little hole. I always *said* it was a lousy little hole."

He took a pencil stub out of his pocket and held it across the table under the other man's nose, making plucking movements at the air with his hand. With each new movement the pencil disappeared or reappeared. "Strictly one horse. Stinking little one horse."

He took a long drink. "Where'd they go, Lonnie?" he said imperiously. "Where'd my wife and kids go?"

"They got on the night train. That's all I know."

"A great thing," Sondern said heavily. "A great thing."

"How'd you happen to come back here after all that time?" Rivers asked.

"There's no law. There's no law at all."

"No, hell no, but it must be three-four years since they came here."

"There's no law."

"What are you going to do?"

"Do?" Sondern shook his head vacantly. Then he said splendidly, "I'll do what I want." His voice sank to a cunning whisper: "What do you suppose they'd say if I went back to the bank? Went back to the bank as manager. Ran the whole shooting match? What do you suppose they'd say about that?"

"I thought the bank let you out," Rivers said brutally.

Sondern went on as though he had not heard. His voice suddenly rose to a shout. "Well, they don't need to worry about that. They could come to me on their bended knees!" He got up from his chair again and walked unsteadily to the kitchen window and looked out across the street. "They haven't even got their sign painted," he said contemptuously. "Hey, who's that?"

Rivers came to the window and looked across the sunlit morning snow. "That's Mr. Ellis. Remember, I told you Dobbs retired. Mr. Ellis has got the bank now."

"Mister Ellis," Sondern mocked. "Mister Ellis. Look at him."

Abruptly he lurched back to the table and scooped up the strewn cards. He rushed to the door and flung it open and raced bareheaded for the other side of the street. "Hey!" he yelled, "hey you!"

Lonnie Rivers stood at the door bawling after him in alarm. "Come on back here. You come back." Sondern slipped and fell heavily in the packed snow in the middle of the road. But he got up again and raced the rest of the way to his quarry, now standing poised uncertainly at the bottom of the cement steps leading up to the entrance to the bank.

He thrust the cards in the hypnotized stranger's face. "Take a card, you smart bastard," he yelled. "Take any card!"

Chapter Four

Mrs. Sondern's faith was of that dogged kind which, meeting many assaults and rebuffs, builds immunities. She had sensed, long ago, that to allow her faith to waver was a luxury she could not afford. She had developed, quite unconsciously, a technique for isolating the separate incursions against her faith and dealing with them one by one. No one problem had anything to do with any other problem, no one year had anything to do with any other year and no one hour had anything to do with another hour. Everything, either in terms of time or of problems, was parceled into compartments. The closer she could bring herself to admitting that things were not going well in any one compartment, the more certain she was that things were going well, or would go well, in the adjoining compartments.

Now as she stood on the station platform at Elevator, there were three compartments to consider. In one lay the problem of finding a place for them to live; in another the need of keeping the children apart from their father; in a third the need of pressing on.

"My, smell that sky," she invited the children. "Just smell that sky."

Harold, impervious to the crystal beauty of the new winter day, was blowing on his fingers through his mitts. There was nothing left of the brief exaltation he had known a few hours before. He surveyed the platform glumly and sheepishly, a dupe of the scented night mocked by an unbeguiling morning. "Where are we going to go?" he muttered.

Kally was rolling a snowball. A small boy, the only other person left on the platform, had approached to within a few steps and was studying them with hostility and suspicion. Kally threw the snowball at him. He crept away. "Now, Kally," Mrs. Sondern admonished.

"Where are we going to go?" Harold repeated.

"Why we're going to stay right here for a while," Mrs. Sondern said. "It's such a long trip that we'd better stay right here for a while."

"To recroup our modest fortune," Kally said, and giggled good-naturedly.

Harold stared bitterly at his sister. "But *where*, Mother?"

Mrs. Sondern patted his red cheek. "Old Mr. Worry Wart," she said affectionately. "I think we'd better just step into the waiting room and sit for a while."

"And plan our straddegy," Kally said importantly.

Mrs. Sondern picked up the scuffed black club bag. Kally took the handle of the wicker suitcase and jiggled it impatiently until Harold, deep in anger for her flightiness, thrust one hand beneath the rope which encircled its bulging middle, and began half dragging and half carrying it toward the nearby depot door. A wave of heat enveloped them as they entered the big square high-ceilinged room, bare of furniture except for a U of slatted yellow benches arranged against three of its walls. The station agent, working behind a wicket leading to the inner office, looked up briefly and returned to a stack of papers. Instinctively they shuffled to the furthest, most secret corner of the empty room.

"Well!" Mrs. Sondern said. She had spoken quietly enough, but the word vaulted into the high bare room with the naked abruptness of an infidel's oath shouted in a cathedral. "Well!" She apologized by repeating the word in a whisper and smiling weakly at the man behind the wicket.

"Why don't we go back to Dobie?" Harold whispered.

"Now, Harold, that's silly," his mother whispered back. "We're nearly a hundred miles closer right now than we were this time yesterday. Even if we *wanted* to go back, it would be a terrible waste of money."

"We'll never get there," Harold mumbled.

"Oh, Harold!" Kally sniffed. "You make me sick."

"Sure!" he hissed with the beginnings of anger. Then on a wild, savage impulse, he leaped from the bench and ran across the room to the ticket wicket. His voice trembling before his own unprecedented daring, he shouted through the wicket at the station agent: "Please, mister, can you tell me how far it is to Grande Prairie, Alberta?"

The man looked up, mildly startled, but in a not unfriendly way. "Lessee now," he said. "That'd be on the Northern Alberta out of Edmonton. Quite a few people from around here went up there two, three years ago. A cousin of mine, he did real well. Well now, lessee. You'd get out of here to Moose Jaw. Moose Jaw to Calgary. Calgary to Edmonton. And then maybe another five, six hundred miles. Just a minute. I'd say—oh, about seventeen, eighteen hundred miles."

"And what would the fare be?" Harold shouted, almost weeping with triumph and despair. "What would the fare be for three people?"

His mother, at first as stunned by his wild self-assertiveness as Harold himself, had crossed the room and grasped him by the elbow. "Please don't bother," she smiled to the

station agent. "We can find out again." Harold did not protest. He went uncomplainingly back to the corner, limp with
the relieved bravado of one who has asked, fair and square,
to hear the worst and has not been told it.

"They have excursions, you know," Mrs. Sondern whispered. "And half fares. It won't cost nearly as much as a
person might think."

"Of course not!" Kally hissed.

Harold stared at a disk of melting snow on one of his
dubbined shoepacks. "But what are we going to do in the
meantime?" he demanded stubbornly.

"Well, that's better! That's much better. One thing at a
time is what I say."

"Let's go to the hotel," Kally urged.

"Now that's a very good suggestion, Kally," Mrs. Sondern
announced. "Of course, you can't be too sure about hotels.
Sometimes they have bedbugs." She was still not in the least
doubtful of her ability to solve the immediate problem, once
she got a fair chance to think about it.

Just then the doorway to the platform gulped open. CPR
Chatsworth, the conductor on the train which had brought
them, paused in the entrance, pressing on the door with his
back until it overcame the resistance of its hydraulic hinge
and wheezed shut again. He had changed his peaked conductor's cap for a black Persian lamb astrakhan. He wore a
long black overcoat and carried a small black valise. His long
heavy-featured face was now even more doleful. He approached them with the soft hushed steps of a doctor entering a sickroom.

"I just thought," he sighed, and let the sentence lie there.
He unbuttoned his coat and took an immense yellow Wal-
tham watch from the pocket of his vest. He studied the
watch. "I just thought as long as I was going uptown I might
give you a hand with your bags."

"That's very kind," Mrs. Sondern said. "We were just sort of . . ."

"I didn't want to mention it before," Mr. Chatsworth said, turning the watch over in his big hand, "but I thought if you hadn't made up your minds about where you were going to stay . . ."

"That's very kind."

"I mean we've got a couple of extra rooms. Just the wife and I and we've got these rooms."

"We'd more or less made up our minds to stay at the hotel for a few days. Only until my husband comes, of course."

"Yes," he said. "It's just that with a big house to heat and coal what it is."

"That *is* a point," Mrs. Sondern agreed.

"You could try it for a few days," he suggested. "And if you didn't like it, it wouldn't need to cost anybody anything."

The poor, poor man, Mrs. Sondern thought. Why, he's worried sick.

"I couldn't hear of it," she said in her friendliest way.

"Well . . ." Mr. Chatsworth said abjectly.

"Oh, my goodness." Her beam of impetuous, faintly impatient magnanimity embraced them all. She rose. With the forlorn eagerness of an old Saint Bernard dog investigating a strange and faintly belligerent cat, Mr. Chatsworth approached the wicker suitcase, made two or three feints at it with his large red hands and finally found a satisfactory grip beneath its rope girdle. He handed his own small bag to Harold. Mrs. Sondern picked up the black club bag. They went out the door in that order, Kally bringing up the rear empty-handed.

They walked in silent procession to the end of the station platform and then turned up the main street, still in procession to take advantage of the narrow path beaten by a few earlier risers in the fresh snow. The new town differed

from the town they had left the night before chiefly in details as minor and easily adjusted to as the snow itself. The
square red-brick hotel standing on the corner had a wooden
sign in front that read The Manor Rooms $1.50 Up Best
Quality Meals. Back in Dobie the hotel's name had been
The Palace Rooms $1.50 Up First Quality Meals. Here the
equally square and equally red brick building across the
street was named not Barber and Billiards No Minors, but
Barber and Pool Minors Keep Out. The restaurant was The
Carlton J. Wong Prop, rather than The Strand Prop G. Kee.
The stores were Baker's General, Red and White, and Kar-
puck's Groceries and Dry Goods, in default of Dalyrymple's
General, Red and White, and Wilston's Dry Goods and
Groceries. The other half of the post office was occupied not
by Bank of Montreal Est. 1817 but by Royal Bank of Canada
Est. 1869.

There were no other significant variations between this
town and the other; brown wooden false fronts on the stores,
canned soups, boys' sweaters, calico dresses, Lowney's Nut-
Milk Bars and Fels Naptha Soap lurking beneath the green
partly drawn blinds; the yellow steeple of the United Church
poking skyward at the top of the street; further on, the high
board fence guarding the fair grounds and after that the
prairie, clean shining snow and winter-blackened poplar
bluffs. It was the small town of Saskatchewan, a town much
idealized by those who have never lived there, much moved-
away-from by those who have, and much mourned by people of both kinds. Before she was halfway up the street Mrs.
Sondern felt the town settling around her plump person as
easily and familiarly as an old girdle. "My, what a lovely
place!" she said.

The difficulties of orienting to their new home proved me-
chanical, rather than spiritual. The front vestibule of Mr.
Chatsworth's house, like the wooden two-story dwelling itself, was a good deal larger than the average of the similar

dwellings around it and they all crowded into it behind Mr. Chatsworth, banging their snow-covered feet and awaiting their turns with the worn V-headed snow broom which stood just inside the entrance. While Mr. Chatsworth was bent over the bags, arranging them near the inner door leading into the house, the face of a woman appeared on the other side of the door, visible only in its outlines through a pane of purple glass. Mrs. Sondern perceived instantly that Mr. Chatsworth could not be seen by the purple woman on the other side of the door; she saw the need of directing the woman's attention somehow to his presence and his sponsorship. "Harold!" she said, in a voice which she tried to make casual and informal and still hearty enough to penetrate to the other side of the door, "Give Mr. Chatsworth a hand with the bags." Harold was more than willing. To him, the surprised lavender gape of the woman inside was belittling and accusing, and in his haste to disengage himself from it he flew to Mr. Chatsworth's aid as though flung from a catapult. "Let me!" he croaked at Mr. Chatsworth's hunched-over back. He shot a determined fist under the man's nearest armpit and began clawing gallantly for possession of the wicker suitcase. Mr. Chatsworth had by now almost succeeded in balancing the suitcase on one of its rounded, over-stuffed ends. But under Harold's anxious assault he and it fell in opposite directions, each with a thump. In the same instant Kally, who had been occupied with the snow broom, caught her first glimpse of the purple visage behind the door, now frozen in a mask of bewilderment. "Look out!" Kally screamed. "There's a *face* in there!"

Altogether, the situation took a fair amount of sorting out and explaining. It turned out, fortunately, that Mrs. Chatsworth, although plainly outraged by the whole proceedings, had one of those thirsty but unassimilative minds which never pause to catch up with themselves. Her curiosity kept galloping ahead of her emotions; it no sooner supplied her with a cause for disbelief or indignation than it caught the spoor of a cause for suspicion or resentment and went view-hallooing in another direction. If Mr. Chatsworth intended bringing visitors, why couldn't he have telephoned from the station? Oh, boarders, but they hadn't had boarders for—— Why, at least, hadn't he rung the bell or opened the door before banging and plunging around like that and scaring everybody half to—— What was wrong with that railroad anyway, three hours late last trip, nearly seven hours this trip, you'd think they'd—— If Mrs. Sondern and the kiddies were going on to Alberta anyway, not that they weren't perfectly welcome, but the one-fifteen to Moose Jaw—— No wonder the poor child started screaming; she must have had the impression the house was supposed to be empty, but how in the world did he ever succeed in giving her that idea—— Well, yes, if it was just a matter of a few days until the gentleman came on from Dobie, they would probably find it comfortable enough; although even with the back upstairs more or less self-contained, two children and *two* adults might find it just a little——

Mrs. Chatsworth stood in the inner hallway, a small gray study in frustration, a woman so much put upon that her wrongs defied articulation. Her husband towered gloomily above her, turning his watch over and over in his hand and speaking to her, when required or permitted, in tones of soothing melancholy. At last she said helplessly: "Well, I expect you'll want to go up." She led Mrs. Sondern and the children through a large clean kitchen to a back stairway which led to a small self-contained apartment on the second floor. "Bedroom sleeps two," she said. "One can use the couch. Kitchenette's back here. Septic in the basement. I'll bring up bedding later. I hope you'll be comfortable."

"It's just real nice, thank you," Mrs. Sondern said. After Mrs. Chatsworth had left, she repeated it. "It's just real, real nice."

After they had unpacked, Kally went back down the main street to the Red and White store and bought some tinned beans, a loaf of bread, and a tin of cocoa for their lunch. They lingered over their seconds of cocoa and conferred. It was agreed, unanimously, that their new home was so fine they need feel in no urgent haste to move further onward. To this a rider was attached, also unanimous, that their ultimate purpose and ultimate destination remain unchanged. Motion passed, Harold dissenting, that there was no reason why Mrs. Sondern shouldn't help some of the ladies of the town with their washing if such help was needed. Motion passed, Harold abstaining, that the local possibilities of the needlepoint industry should be investigated as soon as feasible. Motion passed, unanimously, that Mr. Chatsworth was a real nice man. Motion passed, Kally dissenting, that Mrs. Chatsworth was a nice woman. Meeting adjourned with singing, *sotto voce* but vivaciously, Harold abstaining, of "When The Roll Is Called Up Yonder."

Chapter Five

Had he lived in a time when men looked on Christian martyrdom as anything but comic and preposterous, CPR Chatsworth might well have fed the lions in the Colosseum or, quite as joyously, perished in an auto-da-fé in Madrid. As it was, he represented an anachronism: a man lacking neither in conviction nor, in at least some measure, the courage of conviction; but a man still cheated, vitiated, and disarmed by the lack of opportunities to try his convictions out.

He had never, except in his very early childhood and in one brief, cruel paroxysm when he was past the age of forty, sought to find a formal religion. He had simply hoped to live by the golden rule and, if not precisely to be honored for doing so, at least to be taken seriously. This, through personal limitations which he understood just well enough to increase his torment, proved impossible for him.

When he was still very young the mother who had first instructed him in the matter died, with a final reminder that the most important thing in life was Doing Good to Others. It was about the same time that his father, up to then a tentatively committed do-good man himself, sud-

denly became bankrupted and disgraced through the pro-
longed and skillful dishonesty of a trusted business partner.
The senior Chatsworth was nearing forty-five before he had
paid off his debts and felt free to move west and begin again
as a farmer. With a nine-year-old son to raise and a section
of new wheatland to break, he advertised in the paper for
another wife, went to Winnipeg to inspect the three most
promising and accessible candidates, and selected a strong
and conveniently bewildered Ukrainian girl, whose recently
immigrated parents had just been cremated in a rooming-
house fire. The night they arrived at the farm he introduced
her to young Bill and said crisply, but not unkindly: "Put
hair on his chest."

Throughout his boyhood, Billy Chatsworth's training
and his education fought fearful battles, stained with the
blood of his secret heart, against his instinct and his inclina-
tions. He yearned for nobility and nobility receded like a
choked-off cry.

His father accumulated wealth, or what passed for wealth
in those times and parts. He was still in vigorous health, a
big, florid man who assailed his land with industry and rage.
Toward people—his neighbors and his help—he behaved
with implacable honesty and scrupulous inhumanity. In
good years and bad he paid his stookers and threshers exactly twenty-five cents a day above the going wage, and set
them exact daily quotas which—since he would only hire
especially hard and willing men—gave him the cheapest
wheat in the district and the quickest, cleanest, most prof-
itable harvests. Before long he was threshing his neighbors'
crops on contract. He was not a man for pride, but since he
could not feel pride, he had the need to feel contempt. This
he fulfilled through his ability to do a better job on the soil
than the natives of the soil could do.

In the bad years they turned to him for money. By then
Billy's second mother had died. The boy's only vivid mem-

ories of her were the brisk, unending, cheerful clatter of stoves, brooms, dishes and milk pails and a few gingerly caresses stolen above his father's constant admonitions to "quit treating the youngster as if he was a goddamn doll!"

Every time a neighbor came to seek a loan, or to pay a loan, or to ask for an extension of a loan, Chatsworth made a point of conducting the transaction in the boy's presence. During the second decade of his life young Billy came to know the story of a dozen failures with the same impersonal and academic intimacy that a professional theatrical critic will acquire toward a familiar play in which he has heard many varied readings of the same lines. And always his father, like Chorus, kept the moral before him: "See that? They're all alike, by God! Borrow your money, then hate you for wanting them to pay it back!" Billy, of course, grew up hated like his father.

His father died when Billy was twenty-one, leaving a good deal less money than had been expected. Billy sought eagerly to reclaim his kinship with the human race, but he did not know where or how to present his faded credentials. He went through what money there was in one bitter, angry year, trying to buy on the sordid little streets near the railroad yards of Winnipeg the things for which he could not even find a name. He drank and whored in a highly uninstructed, highly disappointing way, and then reformed, found a job on the railroad, and lived a life of exemplary prudence and emptiness until he reached the age of forty.

One night he found himself, almost by chance, sitting in a camp meeting outside the little Manitoba town at the end of his regular brakeman's run. Before the evening was over he was groveling in a pile of straw before a wooden altar while majestic voices spoke inside his head and his own voice thundered piteously for the Lamb to come and claim him. He arose dazed and full of glory just in time to witness the arrest of the presiding pastor on charges of having attempted

rape against one member of his congregation, as well as se-
ducing two others below the age of consent and spending
an inordinate percentage of the collections to acquire a tent
full of illegal booze. In Chatsworth's search for affinity, this
debacle represented the last fling. Men who make fools of
themselves pursuing sin can expect the understanding, if not
the sympathy, of their fellows; but a man who makes a fool
of himself pursuing virtue is beneath anything but ridicule.
This time the moral stuck; at last he was ready to believe if
not quite to abide by the precepts of his father. He asked
the railroad to transfer him to another branch. The request
was granted after his superior—who had heard about the
camp meeting—had read him a lecture on the advantages of
circumspection, particularly to railroad men on small branch
lines.

His marriage, which took place shortly afterward, was a
final surrender to common sense and non-impulsiveness. He
turned, of course, to a woman who negated all his early
yearnings. She was almost as old as he, a sensible near virgin
of thirty-nine, who, his state of defeat and loneliness being
as abject as it was, had the hospitable, reassuring appeal of
a coffin. They got on well enough together, as often happens with couples who have so little in common that there
is no ground for conflict or resentment. Three times a week
Chatsworth made his two-hundred-mile return run on the
railroad. This left him at home three nights and all day Sunday. After the first year the nights were as quiet and virginal
as the Sabbath afternoons. The sense of sinking into a coffin
had been with him for more than twenty years, and now,
sixty-four and nearing the age of retirement, he did not
struggle against it. He had not altogether lost the urge to
struggle, but he could not find the means to struggle. Where
was the enemy? The enemy had disappeared, faded without
a trace, as a nightmare fades in the hollow, sweat-bathed
instant of awaking, leaving the feeling that something ter-

rible was there which cannot be remembered or opposed.

Sometimes, to be sure, a remnant of the old impulse stirred. Sometimes, to be sure, he still wished that he could find a way to create more warmth between himself and his daughter. In the beginning he had not been prepared for parenthood and he had never been able to catch up. Bearing her pregnancy joylessly, lean and guilt ridden, Amelia had not told him of it until the eighth month; Billy, a stranger in the new town and out of town almost all the time anyway, was not the sort of man a strange doctor went out of his way to congratulate in advance. When, a bare three weeks before her confinement, he asked her in bewilderment why she hadn't told him sooner, Amelia replied crossly that it was a man's business to *know* such things. Chatsworth found the accusation so utterly mysterious that he was sure it must be utterly just. He did not question it.

The first few times he heard it said in the child's presence that of course her father hadn't wanted her (*the silly, lucky man, of course he's changed his mind long since*) he offered a feeble demurrer. And one black Sunday afternoon he struck Amelia for saying it; struck her for the darting, clever glance she had made in the child's direction; struck her for their whole life together and the coffin-cry of its summing up: *See, Billy Chatsworth? Even now, I'm all you've got and ever will have! You haven't even got a daughter!* Struck her three times, while the little girl's look of puzzlement and faint hurt changed to hate and terror.

After that his dealings with Vanessa were much like the normal part of his dealings with Amelia: Everything that stood in need or in hope of settlement was now settled. Because it was final, there was no need of further struggle, no further place for expectation or disappointment. During the remainder of her childhood Billy took his daughter to the Chinaman's every Sunday after Sunday school and bought her a strawberry ice-cream cone. On the way to the Chinaman's and back they talked of dolls, of simple arithmetic problems, of domestic animals and familiar food staples, choosing their words cautiously and uttering them in the uncertain, hopeful tones of beginners in a Berlitz class. Vanny was, of course, wildly devoted to Amelia, as was Amelia to her.

The child spent the first month of her eleventh year in bed; a fairly mild case of measles, their family doctor said, complicated—he said later, and with a consummate absence of tact—by too much babying. Amelia refused his advice that the child be evicted from her bed by physical force if necessary. Another doctor gave her the same advice. But Amelia knew her own eyes and her own child and Vanny remained in bed, attended only by her mother. At the end of six months a young physician from Regina came to pay a visit with his parents near town. Amelia sent for him on her husband's unexpectedly dogged insistence.

"How long has she been ill?" the young doctor asked. Billy thought it strange that he asked nothing about the nature of the illness, but then remembered that the doctor was young and from the city and that this was his first professional call in the community where he had grown up, and therefore that he had much to live up to and much more to atone.

"Well," the doctor said, after a lengthy examination. "Well," he repeated carefully. Then he said, in a tentative, guarded way, as though he might or might not be changing the subject: "Did you happen to read that article in Maclean's on rheumatic fever?" He looked quickly at Amelia, as though for a sign of recognition. "My poor baby!" Amelia choked and began to cry.

"Now! Now!" the doctor said, much more confidently. "It's almost a complete recovery already."

Amelia and Vanny read everything they could find about rheumatic fever during the last months of the convalescence.

It all pointed to the same thing: if Amelia had heeded the first two doctors, Vanny would either be dead or crippled for life. But now—thanks to merciful God—there was no need ever to trust a doctor again. All that was necessary was to be careful of Vanny's heart.

Vanny was not allowed to run or skate or dance or swim, although, as her mother thankfully reminded the neighbors, she was able to lead a perfectly normal life in all other respects. Because of the time she had lost, she was almost nineteen before she graduated from high school; but even this had been a blessing in its way, for otherwise she might not have been considered mature enough to be given the one position in the village to which she was ideally suited. This was the position of town librarian. The library was open from noon to nine on Saturdays and from eight to ten on Mondays, Wednesdays and Thursdays; Vanny was able to discharge her tasks without any severe tax on her strength and she still had a good deal of time at home for reading, of which she was genuinely fond. It was universally agreed after the first year that she was the best librarian the town had ever had. She was often referred to as one of the most popular girls in Elevator; it meant, her father was glumly aware, that she had neither a single enemy nor a single friend, that no one coveted her and no one was jealous of her.

Billy himself continued to converse with her in set and stilted phrases, like a form of Berlitz. The only difference now was that they had moved along from dogs and cats and dolls and cakes to the Standard Works of Literature. Now, in her twenty-second year, Billy was really no closer to her than he had been in her second year or her twelfth. The things he knew about her could be encompassed in three or four short sentences. He had never heard her laugh out loud. But she smiled quite frequently, in a kind and patient way. She was very close to being pretty, with a smooth white skin, black hair, and dark brown eyes. Her body, considering that it had been so little used, was surprisingly clean and supple and graceful.

But Billy Chatsworth, better known as CPR Chatsworth, was no longer ambitious for the affection even of his daughter. Respecting the new strangers in his home he had no ambitions either. It had not been a free act of will which had led him to gather in the remnants of the Sondern family. More a reflex, a nervous twitch, which he could neither help nor make sense of. He had pieced together their situation from gossip heard in the few minutes while his train stood beside the platform at Dobie. He knew their desperate need of befriending, but he did not really feel drawn to them. On the contrary he was a little repelled, in the helpless hypnotized way of a reformed drunkard who, seeing an untended bottle, knows the wish to touch it and, having touched, cannot bring his hand away. He did not expect that in the long run he would be able to do anything for them or they for him. Probably they would manage to cheat him in one way or another, just as he himself had cheated Amelia by offering the sanctuary of their coffin to these strangers who had no right to it and were not yet even ready for it. But there were some things a man could not control.

He avoided a scene with Amelia by refusing to discuss the matter with her at all. He avoided a scene with himself by refusing to talk to the Sonderns. During the first week of their tenancy, he entered and left the house with positive stealth; Mrs. Sondern intercepted him once in the front yard and told him gratefully that if it was all the same, her husband had been delayed a while in Dobie and perhaps they'd stay here and have the children finish out the school term. He said it was all the same. Once the child called Kally was playing in the yard with a tennis ball; she yelled, "Catch?" but he pretended not to hear. After a few days the back-stairway door connecting the upstairs apartment to the downstairs was locked and it was as though nobody else was living there at all.

At the end of the first month his wife told him grudgingly: "Well, she paid the rent."

"Uh-huh," he said. His voice showed no interest, but a tingling came over him, as when some unexpectedly good or heroic thing happens in a book.

"She's taking in washing for half the town. I'll say this for her, she's not lazy."

"Uh-huh."

"They'll probably be here forever," she flared.

"Uh-huh."

Chapter Six

The way it happened that Dutch Reiseling became Harold's friend was what Harold's mother would have called a case of silver linings. Privately Harold considered her frequent use of the expression both indiscriminate and unwarranted, but there was no disputing that his friendship with Dutch Reiseling burst right out of one of the blackest clouds he had ever known.

It was now spring and the first crisis was well behind them. It had taken all of Harold's cunning and red-eyed sullenness to arrange it that way, but ultimately it had been so arranged that he began school before Easter and Kally did not begin until after Easter. He was not going through *that* again. He had gone through it once, in their first year in Dobie, and he was not going to go through it again, not, of all places, in this newer, larger, stranger town.

"I don't see why *either* of us has to go to school," he had said stubbornly. "You said yourself we're only staying here until we get the fare."

"That's right, Harold, but it may take a little while and in the meantime . . ."

"We'd *know* how long if you'd only've let me ask what the fare *is*." He was divided by two utterly incompatible urges, the cruel self-hurting urge on the one hand to remind them that the bigger plan was out of the question, and the hungry urge on the other hand to will the plan closer to fruition. The last would be so much better; when they got to where they were going, if they got to where they were going, all these painful things would vanish. The places would be different there, the people would be different there, the things you had to think about would be different there.

"It won't be so very long." His mother spoke with little conviction and Harold knew that all she wanted now was an excuse to have the discussion brought to an end.

"There should be *one* of us here to help sort the laundry and hang it up. At least for the first while."

It was not a small thing that was at stake. It would have been a large thing for any boy almost. In Dobie Harold had never questioned the inevitability of his taking Kally to school. He had known from the first that a small boy who is charged with taking a slightly smaller girl to school for the first time can expect nothing to come of it but agony and shame. This is ordained in the nature of small boys and of small girls. Consider first the boy. He has already been to school himself and has served a hard apprenticeship in newness. His new face has been glared into, at ominously close range, by faces of greater seniority and height. His new shoes have been scuffed, his new sweater pulled out of shape, his new fears quickened, his new ambitions chastised, his new ignorance marveled at and painfully corrected. If the boy be wise and humble, but not too much of either, he will, at the end of a year, have expiated the folly of his newness in at least some degree.

And then, after his year of struggle and atonement, he must throw its fruits aside with the idiotic bravado of a motion-picture martyr waving away the proffered blindfold.

He must go back to another first day of school with this girl in tow; go back, moreover, as her sponsor and her champion; go back as the defender of the indefensible, the supporter of the insupportable, the spokesman for the unspeakable.

It is of little consequence what sort of girl the girl happens to be. It is enough that she be both new and a girl. Each factor multiplies itself by the other. Nor does it matter how she be prepared. Put her in satins and ribbons and she will arouse the disdainful envy of one sex and the jubilant scorn of the other; allow her nose to run and her drawers to show and the very heavens will grow dark with outrage. Whatever you do with her, she will still be strange. Being strange, she will be conspicuous, and being conspicuous, she will be suspect.

Curiously, the girl herself will be exposed to very little conscious suffering. It is inexpedient to do physical violence to girls, and until the new girl's sensibilities have been honed down enough to feel the imprint of oblique stares and furtive giggles, she is apt to be in a clodlike and rather happy daze. Not so the boy. For him the ramparts of innocence offer no shelter. He knows what the rest of them are thinking.

Harold had not studied out his problem in these exact terms, but he was aware of its every shading nonetheless.

"I still think one of us should stay home for a while," he had repeated miserably.

"Well——" His mother's glance was so appraising and yet so sympathetic that Harold was sure she had divined exactly what was in his mind. But his shame was mixed with wild relief. "Well, all right then, Mr. Bossy."

"School-drool-glockamool!" Kally muttered contemptuously. She sounded so vindictive that Harold could not tell for certain whether her feelings had been hurt or not.

"Aw, dry up," he said gratefully.

Their mother went over and stood beside Kally in the wonderful way she had of taking any little unavoidable wrong that one of them did to the other two and making it appear that the two would soon find a way of doing a little wrong to the one and therefore that there really need be no wrong, or hurt or sense of guilt anywhere. "Boys," she announced, consoling all three of them, "are silly."

So Harold went to school alone, with good will on all sides. Kally went a month later. The small sufferings which are written into the contract evaded neither of them. But they were not suffered jointly, and therefore they were not compounded. Harold had been right all along.

His friendship with Dutch Reiseling came about as an indirect result of one of the small schoolyard torments. One day, after four, there were five kids playing scrub and after they had settled the arguments about who batted first—Harold, of course, was to bat fifth—Rouge the Red Taylor said grandly: "I'm Babe Ruth!" The other boys caught the spirit of it at once. Charlie Johnson echoed: "*I'm* Lou Gehrig." "I'm Carl Hubbell," Buster Jones announced. "I'm Satchel Paige," Jimmy Ryan shouted. "Satchel Paige is good enough for me."

Then they were all looking at Harold with impatient pity. It wasn't just a case of all the good names being gone; all the names of any kind were gone. If his life had depended on it, Harold could not have thought of another major-league ballplayer, past or present.

"I'm Dutch Reiseling," he declared hopefully. Instantly he perceived that it had been an inspiration. The others glared at him, wild with jealousy and rage.

"You *can't* be Dutch Reiseling!" Rouge the Red Taylor's voice fairly trembled with his anger at not having thought of it himself. "Dutch Reiseling lives right here in Elevator."

But Harold knew he had them on the defensive and he repeated boldly: "I'm Dutch Reiseling!" The name sang up in his heart like a hymn. Dutch Reiseling, Dutch Reiseling,

Dutch Reiseling. Not a mere name out of a newspaper, not a mere sound out of a radio set, not a dead face in a magazine, but Dutch Reiseling right here in Elevator in the flesh, as alive and close as breath itself.

Dutch Reiseling, who got seventy dollars a week for playing ball in summer and eighty dollars a week for playing hockey in winter. Dutch Reiseling, who would never have to do a tap of work all his life if he didn't want to. Dutch Reiseling who pitched left-handed and batted from either side of the plate and was said to be the only left-handed pitcher in the entire history of baseball who batted cleanup. Dutch Reiseling who struck out twenty in the final game of the tournament at Minot, North Dakota. Dutch Reiseling who hit six homers in a double-header at Weyburn. Dutch Reiseling, a Regina ballplayer right here in Elevator.

"That's just being crazy!" Charlie Johnson shouted resentfully.

"I'm Dutch Reiseling," Harold repeated proudly.

Dutch Reiseling, who was six feet tall and as dark and good-looking as a cowboy in the movies. Who was as tough and chivalrous as a knight. Who once said gently to a drunk who was determined to fight him: "Let's twist wrists instead," and who twisted the drunk so easily that the drunk sobered up out of sheer terror of what Dutch might have done to him and so went on his way undamaged. Who once, when another man called him a goddamn Kraut, looked hurt for just a moment and then smiled and said: "As a matter of fact, there's also some Polack blood in me and I'm also part Hunky and I've got a little Cree; wouldn't be a bit surprised if there's a little Chinee knocking around too." Who said it so straight and simply that it made the other man look like a fool and made all who heard think just for a moment that perhaps it really was possible for all people everywhere to be friends; who then erased his gentle smile and knocked the other man's goddamn block off.

And who was capable, sometimes, of the most terrific bragging, especially where girls and ladies were concerned. Who was still called The Handsome Stranger to his face by the bold ones, even though he had been in Elevator now for almost a year. Who looked at the timid ones respectfully, but with affection, so that even a kid could tell the girl or lady had never been born that Dutch Reiseling didn't like. Who slept all morning and stood all afternoon beside the billboard outside the Chinaman's, lounging in the sun, waiting for evening ball practice, watching the people go by, laughing and joking and bragging with the men, patronizing and teasing the kids in an easy, good-natured way, singing little half-audible snatches of love songs for the girls and ladies going by, not really fresh but just loudly enough that they could hear and still pretend not to hear if they wanted to.

"I'm Dutch Reiseling!" Harold shouted triumphantly.

The jealousy of the other boys now turned to hatred. "We'll *see* about that!" Rouge the Red Taylor cried in a vengeful fury. "We'll see what *Dutch Reiseling* says about it." He advanced on Harold.

"What you gonna do, Rouge?" Charlie Johnson demanded excitedly.

"We're gonna march this kid right down to Dutch Reiseling and tell Dutch all about it. This kid that can't hit the side of the barn, this kid that's got a wing like a sparrow, this kid that's always falling over his own feet—this kid calls himself Dutch Reiseling! That's what we're gonna tell Dutch Reiseling!"

"Oh boy! Will old Dutch get a laugh outta that!" Charlie Johnson yelled. The other two boys chimed in with whoops of derision and delight.

Harold's splendid world turned to a place of sudden terror. He would have tried to run away, but his knees were too weak. "Gee, fellas," he gulped contritely, "I was only fooling. Honest. I don't wanta be Dutch Reiseling!"

"You should have thought of that before," Rouge the Red said implacably. "Grab him, guys!"

He did not struggle as they marched him down the street toward the Chinaman's; his only hope now was that by some miracle Dutch Reiseling would not be in his accustomed place beside the billboard and that before they could find him elsewhere some second miracle might appear. But when they passed the church steps he could see the place by the Chinaman's quite clearly. Dutch Reiseling was there beside the billboard all right, already in his baseball uniform for the evening practice; worse still, two or three other men had paused to talk with him on the way home from work. His humiliation before Dutch Reiseling, Dutch Reiseling's well-merited hilarity and reproof, were to be witnessed not merely by Harold's own contemporaries but by representatives at large of the august and responsible world of grown-uphood. He did not have the strength to weep.

Dutch Reiseling and the other men glanced up as Rouge the Red tightened his hammer lock on Harold's right arm and thrust the victim within their ken. "Hey, Dutch!" Rouge the Red yelled confidently, "you wanta hear something real funny?"

"Later," Dutch said easily. "Right now *I'm* telling something funny. Let go of that kid's arm," he commanded as an afterthought. "And all you kids go on down the block till I finish this story."

The other boys kept close to Harold as they all walked away. It hadn't been necessary. Harold was still far too terrified to think of flight. In a minute there was a burst of laughter from Dutch Reiseling and the other men. Then one of the men said to Dutch: "Well, can't stay here forever." Another said: "Well, I guess the battle-ax is waiting." And these two men departed, leaving Dutch Reiseling alone by the billboard with the third man, a thin saffron-colored young man, who seemed to slant in several directions like a very old woodshed or a very old icehouse, eyes slanting one way, grin another, knees slanting back and forth and sideways all at once and no use saying it was impossible because it was so.

"All right, you kids!" Dutch Reiseling called down the street. "What's eating you?" The boys started forward, full of eager outrage and expectancy, herding Harold before them. Harold was now so terrified of finding himself in the immediate presence of Dutch Reiseling that he ran toward Dutch Reiseling with the helpless haste of a bird greeting a snake and so outdistanced the other boys by several paces.

"Stop!" Dutch Reiseling called. "Freeze!" Dutch Reiseling shouted. "Don't a one of you kids move another step!" Dutch Reiseling yelled. All the boys, including Harold, stopped. They froze. They did not move another step.

"What's going on here?" Dutch Reiseling demanded sternly. "This kid is scared. Why should this kid be scared?" This was even worse. Harold would gladly have admitted that he was stupid, that he was mouthy, that he was thoroughly feeble, despicable, and mendacious, but he desired as much as he desired life itself to deny that he was scared. "I'm not scared," he tried to protest, but the syllables would not take shape. They stayed far back in his throat, as heavy and unmanageable as so many globules of castor oil.

Dutch Reiseling took a step toward them. The inquiry was about to begin. All the brief postponement had accomplished was to add a new indictment, to create a new dimension for his shame.

But when Dutch Reiseling was half a dozen steps away from Harold and two or three dozen steps away from the other boys he, too, stopped and froze. "Hey!" he said softly to the slanting young man. "Hey!" The slanting man moved to his side. Dutch Reiseling nodded his head very slightly,

so slightly that Harold could detect the hint of movement but the boys further away could not. "Hey!" Dutch
Reiseling whispered to the man beside him. Harold could
barely hear and the other boys could not. "Who's *she?*"

On the far side of the street and two blocks up, just opposite the church steps, Vannie Chatsworth was walking
home from one of her very rare visits to the post office. She
was wearing a plain brown dress, too long, and her black
hair was braided, too thick. But in spite of this she was a
far from ordinary sight. Her skin was white and pink but
not too much of either, like caragana blossoms in the morning sun, and although she carried herself self-consciously and
with excessive carefulness, there was still a grace and flow
to the way she walked.

"Who's *she?*" Dutch Reiseling whispered.

"Ha!" the slanting man mocked him. "Ha!"

"Who *is* she?" Dutch Reiseling grabbed the slanting
man's arm.

"Don't waste your time."

"Who *is* she?" Dutch Reiseling squeezed hard on the
other's arm.

"Cut it out. Vannie Chatsworth." The other man spoke
quickly and aggrieved, in pain. Then he added, atoning for
his weakness after Dutch Reiseling had removed his hand:
"You'll never get *near* her. You'll never Fix *Her* Up."

"Mind your own business," Dutch said. Vannie Chatsworth was now directly opposite, on the other side of the
street, still bearing herself as cautiously as a contestant in
an egg-and-spoon race, but still with a certain flow and
lissome grace.

> "The Sheik of A-rabee
> Your love belongs to me,"

Dutch Reiseling sang, not bigly or obtrusively, but lightly
and half kidding himself so that anybody across the street

could take its hearing as an address or an accident, depending on the person's mood. Vannie Chatsworth did not stir her head.

"See?" the slanting man mocked.

Dutch Reiseling seemed hardly to hear. His eyes were following Vannie Chatsworth down the street. "Jesus-Jesus," he whispered.

"Just try to talk to her! Just talk to her. Even say hello to her. She's sick, you know. She's got a bad heart. Her old lady will call the cops."

"Stop bothering me," Dutch Reiseling said.

"You'll never never *never* in Christ's world Fix *Her* Up!" the slanting man hissed with the fierceness of satisfied envy.

"No?" Dutch Reiseling said. He was still watching Vannie Chatsworth down the street, his dark eyes bright and kind and excited, his smile full of radiant confidence like the smile of a benevolent emperor. "No?"

"For five bucks!"

"For five bucks," Dutch Reiseling repeated absently, still keeping his pleased and generous eyes on Vannie Chatsworth.

"But how will I know if you do?" the slanting man demanded.

"Know?" Dutch Reiseling was still watching Vannie down the street and his voice was far away and tender. "Know? You'll know all right. She'll walk different. You'll see her coming down the street someday and she won't walk like that at all. She'll walk like she was leading a goddamn parade. You'll know all right."

"Ha!" The slanting man tried to sound derisive, but it came out more uneasy.

Vannie Chatsworth turned the corner, and for the first time since she had come in sight Dutch Reiseling gave the slanting man his full attention. "It's a bad thing to bet on," he said, suddenly grave. "We've got no right to bet on a thing like that."

"It's a bet." The slanting man's bright slanting eyes turned away, but there was no sign of yielding in them. "It's a gentleman's bet and you made the bet. You can't welsh."

Dutch moved toward him. "All right," he said matter-of-factly, "it's a bet. And if you tell anybody about it, I'll break you in two."

"I . . ." the slanting man began.

"I'll break you in two," Dutch said with awful firmness. "And that's no lie."

"I'm not gonna tell anybody," the slanting man said indignantly. He began to move away. "See you later," he said.

Dutch turned to the boys, suddenly remembering them. "What do you little bastards mean, eavesdropping?" he demanded in alarm. "What did you hear? Tell me what you heard." He raised his arm, scowling. The other four boys looked genuinely blank; they had frozen, as instructed, and had remained frozen, and it was apparent from their expressions that they hadn't heard a thing but Dutch's few bars of song. They had not heard the conversation.

Harold decided instantly and with regret that he must pretend not to have heard either. Listening to Dutch Reiseling talk about her, watching Dutch Reiseling's kind, caressing eyes follow her down the street, he had been so excited and thrilled for Vannie Chatsworth that he had almost forgotten his own peril. He had thought, indeed, of rushing home behind her to be the first to break the news that Dutch Reiseling intended to Fix Her Up. In the troubled second layers of his mind he had seen the pale girl's face light up with wonderment and pleasure; heard her deny that she was worthy of such stupendous good fortune; reassured her and disputed with her and finally convinced her, and thus won honor for himself as a herald in the path of kings.

But now Dutch Reiseling's tone warned him to be more careful. "I didn't hear anything, sir," Harold said.

Dutch looked at him suspiciously. "All right," he said. Then he waved all the other boys toward him. They gathered in a semicircle, pushing Harold toward the front.

"Now!" Dutch Reiseling said, "what's the trouble? What's wrong with you boys anyway?"

"This kid here . . ." Rouge the Red Taylor began.

"Which kid where?" Dutch was now smiling with paternal severity.

Rouge the Red pointed to Harold. "We were over at the school starting a game of scrub. And do you know what this kid said? This kid said . . ."

"Wait a minute," Dutch interrupted pleasantly. "To start with, who *is* this kid?"

"His name is Harold Sondern," Rouge the Red said, quickly. "We were getting ready to start a game of scrub and this kid said . . ."

"Now, now, let's not rush." Dutch studied Harold. "You must be a new boy here in town." His tone became more stern. "I hope you haven't been getting fresh, have you, Harold? If there's anything a new boy in town shouldn't do, it's get fresh." Harold knew that the last vestige of hope was gone. He *had* been fresh.

"How long have you been here?" Dutch Reiseling asked judicially.

Harold could not speak. "Three or four months," Charlie Johnson said.

"I don't remember seeing you," Dutch Reiseling said. "Where do you live, Harold?"

Still Harold could not speak. "At CPR Chatsworth's," Rouge the Red offered.

"What's that?" Dutch Reiseling asked.

"At CPR Chatsworth's."

"Well, well," Dutch said with sudden interest. "Is that so?"

Harold nodded guiltily.

"You must be pretty crowded, aren't you?" Dutch asked in an oddly detached and academic tone.

"No," Charlie Johnson volunteered. "It's a great big house. *They* live on the top floor and the Chatsworths live below."

"Well, well," Dutch said. "How many people altogether?"

"Him and his sister and his mother," Charlie Johnson said. "And Mr. and Mrs. Chatsworth and Vannie."

"Mr. and Mrs. Chatsworth and Vannie Chatsworth," Dutch said. "Well, well." Harold stared at his feet. He could not guess what new crime he had become involved in; the suspense had grown so awful that he almost wished they would tell Dutch Reiseling about his abortive act of humbug and get that part of it over at least.

"Well!" Dutch repeated sternly. He glared at Rouge the Red and Charlie Johnson and Buster Jones and Jimmy Ryan and then he put his hand on Harold's shoulder. "You other kids bugger off," Dutch Reiseling commanded imperiously. "Me and Harold are going to have a little game of catch."

Chapter Seven

Chris Sondern could not get away from Dobie. Lying on the couch at Lonnie Rivers' late that first afternoon, he had known that he must get away and he had resolved to get away and he had meant, honestly, to keep his resolution.

After Lonnie, too horrified to be really reproachful, had wrested him away from the astonished banker, Mr. Ellis, and led him back across the street, there had been one of those curious twilight times, the dip in the last wave between stupor and oblivion, the absurd, unreckoned half hour of lucidity preceding total darkness. Lonnie, although experienced in such matters, mistook the symptoms for another avocational phenomenon known as drinking-yourself-sober and for a while they talked together on terms of deep sympathy and respect. Of the actual conversation, Chris remembered very little. But he got the impression, strong and unbearably sad, that the people he had come to Dobie to see and whom he had driven away from there would always be remembered in this tiny unsplendid place in a way in which he, their husband and their father, could never be remembered in any of the places of the earth.

"Everybody thought mighty highly of them," Lonnie had said. "At first they puzzled people, but, after, everybody thought mighty highly of them."

That was the thing that made it so necessary for him to go away. They could not have left so very much behind them here, considering the circumstances of their arrival and their departure. But if he diminished what they had left behind them, then he would also be diminishing what little there could have been for them to take away. The longer he stayed here, the more he must diminish both these things; there would be this frail, struggling little plot of esteem and hope and confidence that they had created here, and there he would be, stumbling across it with his drunken feet and drenching it with his drunken vomit. Soon the memory of them would be desecrated by the memory of him, and when, in whatever new crises he had driven them toward, they sought to draw on what they had left behind them for strength and comfort they would find nothing which was not soiled and false.

Lonnie would not recognize how important it was for him to go away. "Lonnie, for God's sake help me up." "No, Chris, you're not in shape." It was this necessity of leaving something somewhere, some good clean feeling, that was so hard to get across with people who had never been in a spot like this. Bea would know. She must have known that no other thing could ever have induced him to follow them here. And only because of knowing it would she have gone away and left him there, without giving him a chance to strive for this better, cleaner feeling between them and him. I love you, Bea. If you'd only stayed long enough to say that you loved me. God damn it, Bea, I'm going to DIE.

"Lonnie, please help me up. I've got to go." Now he was cheating again, trying to put just a little of the blame on her. Perhaps she *had* said she loved him before she left. How could he know? All he remembered was the blur of frightened faces. Bea could put her soft cheek against his right this minute and say that she loved him and promise that she would teach Kally and Harold to love him. But what difference would it make? He'd forget it by the time he woke up and there would be nothing but another blur.

"Lonnie, I've got to get out of here."

"Later, Chris. You're not in shape yet."

"I've got to."

"Listen, Chris, if you went to China it would suit me fine. But I can't have you going out of my place like this in broad daylight. After what you did to Ellis I'll be lucky if the cops aren't around anyway."

"All right, Lonnie. That's fair enough. But I've still got to get away."

He almost did get away, that same night. He awoke a couple of hours after dark and by now Lonnie was ready to let him go and wishing that he would go. He was fine. In the street outside he heard a loud familiar ringing of cowbells and a mighty beating of two-gallon lard pails and the supplicating voices of a dozen small boys pacing up and down the winter night in twos and threes and crying: "Hockey match tonight! Hockey match tonight!"

"Who's playing?"

"Carsvale."

It came to him at once that here, ready-made, was his way of getting out of town while the knowledge that he must get out was still clear and strong. Carsvale was the next village to the east. After the game, according to the inflexible custom of all visiting hockey teams in those parts, the Carsvale hockey team and the half dozen carloads of supporters who had accompanied it would dissolve from the rink and then reassemble on the main street. There would probably be a short interlude while the largest, noisiest, and most belligerent male resident of Carsvale and the largest, noisiest, and most belligerent male resident of Dobie stepped out into the middle of the main street and pummeled each other with their fists until one or both collapsed in the snow and any affronts, injustices, or other issues of civic honor arising from the hockey game could be considered settled. After that, the abstemious members of the visiting party would step into the Chinese restaurant for Denver sandwiches, raisin pie à la mode, and coffee, and the rest would step into the bootlegger's. Before long they would all go home in caravan. There was certain to be room somewhere for a hitchhiker.

Chris kept his decision to himself. Keeping it to himself gave him a twofold satisfaction. He knew he would be doing a worthy thing, so worthy a thing that he did not want to spoil the savor of it by being drawn into a discussion of what he would do once he got to Carsvale. And he saw that Lonnie was beginning to worry. He could almost read Lonnie's thoughts; Lonnie was beginning to be afraid now, afraid that he would never really go of his own volition. And yet Lonnie was not yet quite ready to order him out. Chris knew, almost to the milligram, how much moral courage it takes for a bootlegger to eject a drunk who has gotten drunk on the premises, and Lonnie was a good two or three hours away from building up the necessary head of steam. Good: Let him worry, let him sit there stewing right until the last minute. Then Chris would get up and put on his coat and say, "So long, Lonnie." That way, all the initiative and all the dignity would be on his side. He would go away from Dobie forever and nobody would be able to say that he had gone away a moment sooner than he was ready.

He found another dollar bill and sat playing cat and mouse with Lonnie, ordering another drink of wine, nursing it, ordering another and nursing it, very careful not to get wholly drunk again, but too proud to let Lonnie suspect he was afraid of getting drunk. Everything went according to schedule. In what seemed like a very short time Lonnie's kitchen began to fill up with strangers, most of them, as he had known they would be and was able to confirm from what they were saying about the hockey game, from Carsvale. A little self-conscious about his frayed clothing, Chris had moved to a dark corner of the room when the first of the newcomers entered. They nodded at him without seeming to take notice and he was entirely certain that there would be no difficulty about getting a ride to Carsvale.

While he sat in his corner of the pleasantly noisy room finishing his drink, a tall bulky man in a fleece-and-canvas overcoat came and stood in front of him. The man lowered a pair of round jovial cheeks and a pair of friendly, blue humorous eyes to the level of Sondern's eyes and exclaimed heartily: "Well, for God's sake! Chris Sondern! I heard you was in town."

"Yes," Chris said uneasily, peering into the friendly, humorous eyes.

"Roxy Brannick," the other man shouted. Chris remembered him now, a successful farmer who lived three or four miles north of town. They had had some dealings when Chris had worked here in the bank. They shook hands.

"What are you drinking?" the big man invited. He looked at the nearly empty tumbler in Chris's hand and laughed in mock horror. "Not that goddamn grape swill!" He turned toward the other corner of the room where Rivers was standing and said: "Two ryes here, Lonnie."

In the old days there hadn't been much call for rye, all wine and beer. A gust of self-reproach swept over Chris. He should have known there'd be rye if he'd only had the sense to ask for it. Brannick was right, that goddamn grape swill just nibbled and lapped at you like a sick cat, stale and musty smelling. Rye took an honest bite at you. "Sure."

As he finished his rye, the Carsvale men prepared to leave. Chris pulled himself to his feet and stood swaying gently in the crosscurrent of two separate panics. He was no longer absolutely certain that he would get to Carsvale and he was not absolutely certain that Brannick would offer to buy him another drink of rye. The only perfect thing would be to get the rye and get to Carsvale both, but that was now impossible. If he delayed his departure a minute longer he would certainly not get to Carsvale and he would still have no certain guarantee of the other drink of rye. He cast a look of helpless malevolence across the room at Lonnie Rivers, who he now perceived had been at fault from the beginning for not telling him about the rye.

"Another rye?" Brannick asked.

"Thanks," Chris said quickly, and sat down again. Something sobbed far inside him, biting deep like the rye, half despair and half relief. Why can't he mind his own business? Now he's made me miss my ride to Carsvale.

He woke up late the next morning in the vacant hired man's room at Roxy Brannick's. Somewhere in the distance he heard quick light footsteps and the clanking of a stove. He had not heard these woman sounds in more than four years. For just an instant the throbbing jumble of his recollections found the perfect, the gloriously impossible recess for them. "Bea!" he cried aloud. "Bea!"

Brannick entered the room almost at once, half dressed, scratching the upper half of his woolen underwear. "Her name's Margaret, but you better call her Mrs. Schmidt. She's been keeping house the last four-five years. Oscar Schmidt's widow, he died."

At first the words conveyed no more meaning than Brannick's face. Brannick helped him by coming closer and inspecting him with his playful blue eyes and saying: "Say, you was good and cut!"

Chris sat up and began feeling around for clothing. "I've got to get out of here," he said. "I've got to get the east train."

"My God, you *are* mixed up. You want the west train."

"No, the east train."

"They went west. For God's sake, you lived around here long enough to know that Elevator's *west*."

"Elevator?"

"You *were* cut. Jackie Coogan came in, Jackie Coogan's the assistant agent, don't tell me you forgot *that* too, and you asked him where they went and he said their tickets were to Elevator."

"Sure, I remember that. I just wanted to know. But I wasn't planning to go there myself."

"You wasn't planning to go? Not much you wasn't planning to go! Me and Lonnie and Jackie Coogan had to throw you down on the floor or you'd have started out walking. Right then and there. A ninety-mile walk at twenty-three below."

He could not be sure that Brannick wasn't taunting him. But this was a matter of small importance beside the terror in his own heart. It was a terror such as he had never known. It was far worse than the terror of the hunted; it was the terror of the hunter, driven on and on through a dark forest, stumbling with exhaustion, his heart filled with love for the trembling creature in the still shadows far beyond.

Their tickets were to Elevator. Brannick shouldn't have told him. Now that Brannick had told him, it would not be enough merely to get out of Dobie. He would have to get out of Saskatchewan, out of the West, perhaps out of the country.

"I've got to go to Halifax," he said.

"Hell, Chris," Brannick said, "you don't want to go to Halifax no more'n a rabbit."

"I've got a brother there. He's a big man there."

"You ain't got a brother in Halifax no more'n a rabbit," Brannick said indulgently.

"If you'd drive me to the station, I could take the east

train to Carsvale and get off there. There's a fellow in Carsvale that owes me forty dollars."

"You mean you'll take the train to Carsvale because Carsvale's where they'll throw you off," Brannick chided him companionably. "There ain't nobody in Carsvale owes you forty dollars no more'n a rabbit."

Sondern found his trousers. "I've got to catch that train, Roxy," he said.

"But what about our contract?" Brannick demanded playfully.

"What contract?"

"You was going to stay here and help me with the chores."

"Are you crazy?"

"Oh, I know I wouldn't get much work out of you. As far as that goes, there's not much to do. But God, Chris, I get sick of sitting around and talking to myself and looking at old lady Schmidt. You'd be doing me a favor."

Sondern plucked nervously at the buttons of his shirt. "I can't stay here," he said stubbornly.

Brannick disappeared into the next room. In a moment he returned with two bottles of beer. He held out one to Sondern. "Haira the dog," he invited.

Sondern knocked it from his hand. The bottle writhed on the linoleum floor like a mobile geyser.

"You don't fool me a bit, Brannick!" Chris shouted furiously. "You're a goddamn drunk and the only reason you want me to stay is that I'm a bigger goddamn drunk and every time you look at me you feel like goddamn Jesus Christ."

"I should break you in two," Brannick whispered. But his red face went soft and helpless like a baby's and his mild blue eyes became two ludicrous pools of tears.

To Chris they were not ludicrous. He felt as though he had come upon an old friend in the fastness of an empty desert. He began weeping too.

"That was a terrible thing to say, Roxy. You're the only man that's tried to be decent to me in five years and I said a thing like that."

"It don't matter," Brannick assured him generously. "It don't matter no more'n a rabbit."

"But I've still got to go, Roxy."

"Whatever you say," Brannick agreed. "I'll get the car out right now. I'll take you to the train and if you want to go to Halifax, I'll damn well put you on the train to Halifax. You can send me the money when you get it."

"No."

"When you start worrying I'll start worrying," Brannick said.

They arrived at the station twenty minutes early and the train was a further twenty minutes late. While they sat in the car beside the platform Brannick opened the glove compartment and produced a twenty-five-ounce bottle of Corby's Little Touch. Chris looked at the bottle in an agony of delight, tingling gloriously with a feeling of sheathed power, his for the using in any way he liked. "Well, just a short one, Roxy." He had never enjoyed a drink so much as that one. It hit his belly with the soaring tumult of an anthem, a mighty, shouted toast to the friendship of two friends, each fully understood and fully understanding.

Four drinks later Chris muttered happily: "God, Roxy, I'm getting drunker'n a horse."

Roxy chuckled. "You ain't drunker'n a horse no more'n a rabbit. What you need's a drink."

"You might just have something."

"Let's start this hayrack up right now and go over Lonnie Rivers' and kick the goddamn door down and drink up every drop in the goddamn place and then beat Lonnie's brains out with the empties."

This was the way to do it. Do it like a lion. None of your grubbing around, alone in dark stale fearsome corners, complaining and apologizing, pawing in your pockets with numb, secret fingers, feeling each precious coin, hardly daring to touch their edges for fear the quarters might betray themselves as nickels and the dimes all shrink to pennies. Do it like a lion! Drink the place dry and beat their brains out with the empties!

"Crank 'er up!" Chris sang.

The winter was almost over before the urge to go away became more compelling than the lazy surcease of staying. Brannick turned out to be an even more leonine friend than he had seemed to be that morning at the station. The conditions of their friendship were as simple as the conditions of friendship among men who meet by accident in trenches or in jails. Each accepted the other for what he was. They were as uncritical and unquestioning of each other as two men marching to a scaffold. They did not really get to know each other, in the sense that they exchanged a large number of confidences irrelevant to their situation; the one relevant thing, which was too obvious to require comment, was that they were going the same way. When they talked it was not much of themselves, but of the unvarying excellence of alcohol in any form, the perfidy of women (no names mentioned), the nesting habits of the Canada goose, the mendacity of the Saskatchewan Grit machine (and the necessity of voting for it), the sagacity of a former Regina hockey and football coach named Alvin Horace Ritchie, the virtues of the old Model T, the depredations of dust, drought, grasshoppers and the mortgage companies, and other universal truths. Often they did not talk at all, but sat silently listening to the radio or playing cribbage. Occasionally Chris did card tricks, which Roxy attempted neither to belittle nor to fathom. "God, Chris! I don't know how the hell you do it!" Roxy would cry admiringly. "Just a knack," Chris would say modestly. "Some people have it and some haven't. Here, take another."

There was just enough work on the farm during the last months of winter to impose a rough order on them. Mrs. Schmidt shortly left in a rage, complaining that she could not be expected to cook for two men who drank more than they ate, and their natural bond of sympathy was doubly strengthened by the outrageousness of her reasoning and the unspeakableness of their own cooking.

Actually they drank with what seemed to them both to be an excess of restraint. "Just enough so a man won't go crazy and not quite so much as to kill him," Brannick said with a self-reproving grimace that did not entirely disguise his pride.

By March Chris had almost persuaded himself that he could remain indefinitely. He avoided going to the village itself any more than was absolutely necessary and on the few occasions when he did go there, he went utterly and ostentatiously sober and came back, not without surprise, the same way. He was convinced, almost, that he had exaggerated the danger of his canceling out, for Bea and the children, whatever Dobie had given them of the things that people give to places and places give, in return, to people.

And then, very late one night, a March chinook was blowing and Chris was lurching down a prairie road toward the mocking, beckoning stars. He did not get far before Roxy overtook him in the Chevvy and took him home, but it was not the distance he had gone that mattered. The direction in which he had gone was west, toward Elevator, and he knew there was no guarantee that he would not go in that direction again. For four years, the four years after they had departed from Regina and he had discovered that they had come to Dobie, there had been scarcely a day when he had not devoted some moment, some stab of torment and self-calumny to guaranteeing that he should never follow them. And yet, through some black unrecollected miracle as profitless to study and as impossible to have circumvented as the scaling of a high, unknown cliff by a sleepwalker, he had left Regina and he had arrived in Dobie. The distance from Regina to Dobie was a hundred and twenty miles. The distance from Dobie to Elevator was only ninety miles.

"Roxy," he begged the next morning, squeezing his thin fingers into the big man's shoulders, "if I ever start out west again you come and get me."

"Sure."

"Sure isn't enough." His thin fingers tore with frantic emphasis into Brannick's arms. "I mean you come and get me any way you have to do it."

"Okay, Chris," Brannick agreed uneasily.

"I mean if you have to kill me."

"Sure. But let's forget it for now."

"I'll sign a paper. I'll sign a paper saying I asked you to kill me."

"Sure, that would fix everything dandy," Brannick growled a little less patiently. "Now let's forget it."

It was another month before Chris brought himself to readiness. It was a complex process, involving many physical factors—the state of the weather, the availability of transportation, and the alcoholic content of the blood stream, which could jeopardize the whole operation by being either a fraction too high or a fraction too low in the hour for action. There were abstract factors, too, all necessary to weigh and examine each morning. None of these could be gauged with precision and on none of them did the gauge read exactly the same on any two successive days. On one day it would seem fantastically improbable that, even if he should set out for Elevator again, he would be able to elude Brannick's pursuit. On another day it would seem that the whole problem was absurdly exaggerated and on another that it was simply not susceptible of a solution; if he could not guarantee and control the course of events while he was here in Dobie, what reason was there to believe he would be able to guarantee and control them from Halifax or even Timbuktu. Often it seemed unreasonable to allow a hypothetical, uncommitted wrong to outweigh an established, existing right. He had a right to stay here with his friend, his good and final friend.

One day in April Brannick took the car to go to a distant farm and make some arrangements about seeding. After he had washed the breakfast dishes, Chris helped himself to two small drinks of rye from the bottle in the kitchen cupboard. In a few moments he knew that he was ready. Ready to do it at last; ready to flee into and lose himself forever in the unknown jungles of the East.

He put on his hat and coat, filled a small vinegar bottle with whisky and put it in an inside pocket. There was a five-dollar bill lying carelessly on a shelf above the kitchen table and his eyes rested on it for a moment, but he did not take the bill. He tore a piece of paper from one of the margins of the new issue of the *Star Weekly* and wrote on it: "Dear Roxy—God bless you. Chris."

He walked into Dobie and after a ridiculously short wait he was lying on a grain door on the rods beneath a boxcar on a way freight traveling east. The train moved fast and purposefully. Close as he was to the rails, it seemed to be rushing past the fence posts at a hundred miles an hour. He took the last drink from the vinegar bottle and listened to the sad, soothing, threnody of the wheels: YouCAN'Tget-OFF—YouCAN'Tget-OFF—YouCAN'Tget-OFF. The chances are this whole train is made up; the chances are he'll highball right through to Souris. Out of Souris tonight, into Winnipeg tomorrow. Pick up a meal in Winnipeg—My God, I'll GET to Halifax! If a man puts his mind to it, he can do anything, it's just getting started that's hard.

The train ground to a stop. The thick red ankle of a C.P.R. water tank was close enough for him to reach out and touch. He knew, because he knew the towns along here, that this town was Carsvale. He got off his grain board and went over and sat down in the warm cinders beside the water tank, waiting for the train to pick up or drop whatever cars had been designated to be picked up or dropped and then resume its journey. After an hour the train had not moved, but Chris was not worried.

Early in the afternoon a brakeman walked down the cinders at the side of the train. When he saw Chris sitting beside the water tank he said to him sympathetically: "Tough luck, Buster!"

"Yeah?" Chris said suspiciously.

"Washout up ahead," the brakeman said.

"Yeah?" Chris said.

"I wouldn't wait here too long if I was you," the brakeman said.

"Who's waiting?"

"Okay, nobody's waiting. But if anybody's waiting they're wasting their time."

Chris glared indignantly at the man's receding back. Smart bastards, tell a person there's a washout, then they're gone on him. You'd think the money came out of their own pockets.

He sat on beside the water tank. He grew, in turn, a little thirsty, a little stiff, and later, in the waning afternoon, a little cold and hungry. But he did not move away. From time to time he glanced anxiously up the track for signs of life around the engine. And then he found himself staring interminably at the side of the boxcar which he had vacated. The boxcar took on a personality. This personality changed through the long, numb afternoon, as did the intentions which lay behind it. Once, although there was no sound from the engine, Chris saw the boxcar move, making a quick, treacherous, little spurt and then, as abruptly and silently, freezing as though turned to stone. He flung himself away from the base of the water tank and leaped to the grain door

beneath the car, quivering with his triumph. He lay there
for a long time and then crept back to his place beside the
water tank. The sun went down and it grew quite cold. The
shape of his boxcar receded into the gloom. Chris was alone
in the night, but he did not dare to move away. It was no
longer a question, solely, of waiting out this particular train.
It was a question of waiting out all the trains in the world.
His hatred of trains had grown so great that he knew if he
surrendered to this one, in which he had so much invested,
he would never find it in his heart to go back at a train again.

A light came swinging down the cinders.

"Look, Buster, I wouldn't kid you. There's a washout."

"Yeah?" Now they're getting ready to move. They've been
waiting for a meet, but now they're getting ready to move
again. He wants to get me out of here, the smart bastard.

"Why don't you go uptown and get yourself something to
eat? I've got half a buck if it's any use to you."

"Yeah?"

"Look, Buster, why don't you go and ask the agent if he'll
let you sleep in the waiting room?"

"Yeah?"

"Oh, what the hell." The brakeman strode off, swinging
the lantern in short disgusted arcs. But a few cars down the
track he stopped and turned around. He came back again.

"Listen, Buster," he said. "Did you ever live anywhere on
this line?"

"Yeah."

"You've been sitting right here beside the track since ten
o'clock this morning. It's now eleven o'clock at night."

"Yeah?"

"Well, if you know anything about this line you ought to
know that two passenger trains were due to go over this track
while you've been sitting here."

"When's the washout going to be fixed?" Chris asked. He
did not listen for the answer. He pulled himself laboriously

to his feet and walked without a word to the Carsvale hotel across the tracks from the railroad station. He put in a telephone call, collect, to Roxy Brannick. "For God's sake come and get me, Roxy," he begged. "And Roxy, bring a drink."

Chapter Eight

After that it was never far from his thoughts that he might at last be reunited with Bea and the children in spite of everything.

Three nights after his return from Carsvale he was slumped perkily in the lap of the leather easy chair at one side of the long kitchen table. His dark eyes rested proudly on Roxy Brannick, stretched out full length on the sofa at the other side of the table and wheezing tentatively in the first stages of a heavy sleep.

"Roxy, you old bastard," he said aloud. "I've drunk you under the table. What do you know about that?"

He reached happily for the brown bottle of Corby's Little Touch and replenished his glass. He said aloud again, this time with magnanimity and affection: "Never mind, Roxy, I know it doesn't count. You must have sneaked a few while I was watering the horses."

Outside, the moon had risen fair and full above the poplar bluff and its pewtered gleam alternately engulfed, merged with, and was engulfed by the coppery, washed-out nimbus of the single twenty-five-watt electric bulb flickering high on the ceiling. The gasoline motor in the back shed was running dry, and the light it served suddenly began to fight for existence with the foolish, frightening gallantry of a decapitated rooster. Now and then the electric light was no more than a faintly quivering filament, and in those moments the moonlight was in full possession of the room. And now and then, as the motor coughed and hacked for breath, the electric light flared with a brilliance greater than had even been intended for it, and in those moments the moonlight was driven back behind the dark line of the poplars. Each time a change occurred in the balance between the light and the moon, all the contents of the room changed in shape and texture and shadows rose and fell and changed places. Chris would have liked to go out and do something about the motor, but Roxy had never showed him how it worked. He felt much too good to go to bed, but he had almost made up his mind that that was what he would have to do when the electric light made a sudden and apparently permanent rally. He studied it warily for a few moments and then, satisfied, poured himself another drink.

He drank it in silent communion with Roxy Brannick, his good and final friend. "Wake up, Roxy!" he shouted companionably when he had finished. "People die in their sleep."

You damned fool, now look what you've done. In the years of drinking in solitude, his reveries had become as stylized as the conversation of elevator operators and barbers. Certain gambits called for certain rejoinders and certain rejoinders for certain ripostes and certain ripostes for certain conclusions. He had made his gambit on death, the most familiar gambit of all; if it had been one of the lesser gambits like, say, the deprivations of poverty, he might have been able to revoke it or to steer it toward one of the pleasanter variations, such as the excellence of wealth. But this one was so old and so settled that the only thing to do was to ride it through.

He reached sadly for the bottle, the fleeting mood of cheerfulness beyond recall. That's the hell of it, nothing comes back once it's gone. Far better there was nothing there to begin with.

O.K., here we go again. He walked into the Athens Café on Eleventh Avenue in Regina, sometime back in the twenties it would have to be. What did the exact year matter anyway? He hung his new Christie on the wall and took a seat halfway down the empty lunch counter. It was the first time he had been in the Athens Café or in any café in Regina for that matter. He was a little surprised that no one else was eating. He was also a little gratified; if he wanted to he could eat here again tomorrow and the day after tomorrow, although with his board paid up a month in advance he'd hardly be that foolish.

He had just been promoted from junior in the Dobie branch to second teller in the downtown Regina branch and this, in a way, was a testimonial banquet to his kind and vigilant gods. He ordered the most exotic, unheard-of combination the menu offered, sweetbreads à la king, glacé parsnips, hashed brown potatoes, loganberry pie, and iced coffee and while he was waiting for his order a very wonderful thing happened, right there in the Athens Café on his first day in Regina. Al Ritchie came in and sat down at the counter half a dozen stools away. He knew it was Al Ritchie, just as he would have known it was Al Ritchie if the whole thing had happened five years earlier. Everybody in Saskatchewan knew Al Ritchie's picture.

Al Ritchie sat down half a dozen stools away. A small wide man with a round, good-natured face sat down beside him. Ritchie said: "Coffee, Leggy?" and Chris knew this other man would have to be Leggy Firbank who wrote "Leging It With Leggy" in the *Star*.

For a while they muttered back and forth about the price of wheat and Charlie Dunning and Jimmy Gardiner, the identical things that were engaging the mutters of the eight hundred thousand other residents of Saskatchewan in those times. And then, miraculously, they were talking about Dynamite Frankie Jenkins. It was a minute before Chris caught on, because they referred to him, with privileged intimacy, merely as Frankie. Chris put down his knife and fork and squinted at his untouched sweetbreads in blissful concentration. Half his mind was occupied with the conversation and the other half was composing a letter to Les Murchison back at the bank in Dobie: Dear Les— Dropped into the Athens for a bite the other day. Al Ritchie and Leggy Firbank were chewing the fat about Dynamite Frankie Jenkins and . . .

"So Frankie wants to hang up, let him hang up," Al Ritchie was saying.

"I'm telling you, Al, it's one hell of a mistake."

"What am I supposed to do? If the club can get me Frankie, I can use him. If they can't get him, I can't use him."

"Frankie never held anybody up in his life. All he wants is a suit of clothes *before* the season starts instead of after."

"Tailor-made," Ritchie amplified scornfully. "Tailor-made. Is *that* something?"

"We need him."

"Look, Leggy, I only coach the club. Go see Piffles. Go see Clare."

"Sure, Al, but you need Frankie. You need him like Hug needs Ruth."

"I need twelve men who can do what they're told," Ritchie said. "Besides, Frankie's brittle."

Chris was writing to Les Murchison: Al doesn't take a thing from anybody. Leggy said he needed Frankie Jenkins like Huggins needs Ruth and Al just grinned and said: "All I need is twelve men who can do what they're told."

"He's brittle all right. You're right there, Al," Firbank said.

"A great boy, though, the best. Give Frankie the bones to go with his heart and I'll take him over anybody. I'll take him over Jim Thorpe or Grange. And I saw them both at their best."

"You're right there, Al. If Frankie only had the bones."

"That's what the average public doesn't understand. The average public sees him barreling through that line, knifing through, and they think there goes a big strong man. Two hundred and ten pounds, at least. Maybe two twenty." Ritchie paused and said hopefully: "What would you say Frankie weighs, Leg?"

"One sixty-eight," Firbank said.

Ritchie sounded disappointed. "Well, you *should* know. But the average public takes him for at least two ten. Maybe two twenty."

"Oh, I wouldn't say that, Al."

"I'm telling you," Ritchie said insistently, "the average public takes Frankie for at least two ten."

"No."

Al Ritchie called aggrievedly down the lunch counter. "Hey, Mac."

Chris broke out in a happy sweat. Well, Les, Al was saying to me . . .

Red with embarrassment and delight, Chris looked Al Ritchie in the eye.

"You know anything about football?" Al Ritchie asked.

"A little," Chris said.

"You ever seen Frankie Jenkins play football?"

"Lots of times," Chris lied.

"By the way," Leggy Firbank cut in, "did you happen to hear us talking just now?"

"I couldn't help hearing a word or two," Chris apologized.

He added as a timid, extenuating footnote: "I was eating my dinner."

"But you didn't hear us say anything about how much Frankie Jenkins weighs?" Ritchie asked.

"Oh no," Chris replied eagerly, not meaning to lie again but sensing that an affirmative would end the conversation.

"O.K.," Al Ritchie said. "Would you mind answering a question for us? If I asked you to guess how much Frankie Jenkins weighs, what would you say?"

Chris studied the matter solemnly. "Two hundred and fifteen pounds," he announced.

"Ha!" Ritchie snorted gleefully. "Ha!"

"A plant!" Firbank said darkly. "By God, Al, you'd cut out your grandmother's liver to win an argument."

Ritchie jumped down from his stool and walked down to Chris, extending a White Owl. "My compliments," he said, his lean face dancing.

"Thanks, Mr. Ritchie," Chris gulped. He put out his hand and said boldly. "I'd like to meet you, Mr. Ritchie. My name's Chris Sondern."

"A pleasure," Al Ritchie said warmly and took his hand. Well, Les, as Al said when we were shaking hands . . .

"I work at the Bank of Montreal," Chris said.

"Good. Fine," Ritchie said. "See you around, Chris."

He walked out, with Leggy Firbank grumbling in his wake. Chris turned a glazed, ecstatic eye to his neglected sweetbreads à la king.

"So that was Al Ritchie."

He actually had to give his head a little jerk to make his eye focus on the waitress who had come up unnoticed with his dessert. He took no particular notice of her, except that she was dark and pretty and wore a clean blue and white uniform. But he was glad she was there to talk to.

"Great guy, Al," he said airily.

"He sure doesn't look much like a baseball player, though."

"Baseball player!" Chris looked for a long, hard moment at her pretty innocent face, searching it in vain for a trace of ill-considered levity. "He's not a baseball player," he said. "He's a coach. He coaches football and hockey."

"Well, he doesn't look much like a hockey player either."

"*Coach!*" Chris said angrily. "Say, are you trying to be funny or something?"

The girl tossed her black hair. "And what if I was?" But there was a tiny edge of hurt in her voice and Chris said hastily: "I just can't understand how you could work here and not know about Al Ritchie."

"Poof!" she sniffed. "I've known about Al Ritchie ever since I was knee-high to a grasshopper. But I still don't think he looks like a football player."

"Coach," Chris groaned. "Coach. Just the greatest coach in Canada. Maybe in the world. They talk about their Warners and Staggs and Mike Roddens and Lester Patricks, but —say, how long *have* you been working here?"

"I'm not so sure it's anyone's concern," she said primly. "But the fact of the matter is, this is my first day."

"You don't say!" Chris stretched out the luxurious words of discovery. "You don't say."

"I do say." She giggled. "And I'll bet I'm not the only hick from Hicksville that's just wandered into the big city."

Chris's sense of dignity skirmished briefly with his need for a confidante, an interim Les Murchison. And then, with a shrug of careless grandeur, he threw away his advantage.

"Dobie. I worked in the bank there. Grew up in Shaunavon."

"Wapella," she said.

"Wapella," he said munificently. "I was there once."

"Is this your very first time in Regina too?" she asked hopefully.

Chris engaged his conscience in a tremendous seethe of battle. "Yes," he admitted gallantly at length. He added quickly, with a worldly grimace: "I can't see so much to get excited about."

"Oh, I think it's fantastic," she said. "Why, the parliament buildings alone, they're absolutely fantastic."

"Yes," he conceded. "They're quite a sight all right. Of course," he blurted with inane worldliness, "they're nothing like Westminster Abbey."

"Have you . . ." The girl paused. Chris glared morbidly at the counter, full of guilt and apprehension and deceit trembling on the brink of judgment. But she did not complete the question. It was in that instant that he began to love her.

Chris was twenty-one. Bea was a few months younger. One night, when Chris stopped in to walk her home to her boardinghouse, Bea said shyly to her employer: "Don't we make a handsome couple, Mr. Lestrous?"

"You make still better," Mr. Lestrous said earnestly. "You make a *couple*."

Chris stole a long glance in the mirror standing behind the glass cash desk. Bea's dark head was turned toward him, Wapella, Saskatchewan, written defiantly on every line of her spring hat, cherry red with a grass-green feather, as bright and confident as a child's first crayon drawing. His own head, carefully brilliantined, hovered stiff and self-conscious above his blue-serge shoulders as though pinioned in an old-fashioned portrait photographer's clamp.

"You mean," Chris stammered lightly, "we've both got straw in our hair."

"Oh, Chris, you say the awfulest things!" Bea giggled, not in the least offended.

"That's good," Mr. Lestrous roared, pounding the top of the cash desk. His chuckling subsided and he said very seriously: "Straw in the hair, maybe. But something big in the heart." Now he was embarrassed too. "Have a cigar, Chris. I got some that's too rotten to sell and not rotten enough to throw away."

Chris was dragging down his eighteen dollars a week with every reasonable prospect of more. It was far below the minimum on which the bank permitted its employees to marry and it was not an easy thing to give it up. At first they kept their marriage a secret and Chris stayed on at the bank while Bea tended their two furnished rooms, but they had known discovery would not be long in coming and when it did come they accepted the consequences without rancor.

Chris miraculously found another job keeping books in a dry-goods store. This one paid only seventeen dollars, but the sum was adequate. After they had been married a year they took a weekend excursion to Winnipeg and ate their anniversary dinner right in the main dining room of the Royal Alexandra Hotel, Bea nervously protesting that the Royal Alex was only for the rich and elegant and they would be turned from the door as impostors. Nothing of the kind occurred; a head waiter in a splendid dinner jacket took them to their table, another waiter in a dinner jacket, equally splendid, brought them food, and a bus boy in virginal white bore away the ruins. Chris left a twenty-cent tip and they went from there to an upstairs palace on Portage Avenue and danced under a firmament of paper stars.

"Roxy!" Chris shouted uneasily across the kitchen table. "Wake up, Roxy. Wake up and talk to me." But the rhythm of Brannick's breathing was sure and unbreakable.

He didn't know what had happened. He had no idea. Policemen, magistrates, clergymen, doctors, one wonderfully sympathetic lady major in the Salvation Army, and, for a year or two, a young intern at the Regina General who was dabbling in this new science of psychiatry, had done what they could to lead him to an understanding of his trouble. From them Chris learned, or at any rate was content to believe, that his own diagnosis was superficial and meaningless. It wasn't enough merely to say that a man drank because he liked to drink, liked the taste and the lift of it. There had to be something deeper, particularly when the drinking ceased to be a pleasure and became a torture and a catastrophe, and yet it still went on.

Chris did his best to co-operate, sometimes driven to it by terror and hopelessness, more often through a desire to be obliging. He knew all along that it wasn't going to get anybody anywhere, of course. It's good of you to see me in your office like this, Your Worship. No, there's nothing wrong between my wife and me, Your Worship. So far as I'm concerned she's the finest woman in the world, and here's the funny thing, she acts as if she still thinks I'm the finest man in the world. No, I don't think ten days will do me any good, Your Worship. I don't think it will do me any harm, but I can't see it doing me any good either. You do whatever you think you ought to do, Your Worship.

Yes, Doctor, it's true. I started hitting it about the time the first one was born. But I don't think there's any hidden jealousy or anything like that. I'm just as crazy about them both as their mother is. I know you'd never know it from the things I do, but I'm trying to give you the best answers I can.

No, Major, I don't think being let out by the bank had anything to do with it. After all, it was nearly three years after that that I started.

So many people were pulling for him, so many things had been running for him. Bea sold silk stockings and magazine subscriptions from door to door. She scrubbed floors and for a while she went back to the Athens. She never reproached him, not a word ever passed between them, she just watched and tended him with pity and stricken fatalism. One night, shortly after Kally was born, she did say to him, very quietly and soothingly: "Chris, we'll soon have to leave you."

He pretended not to hear, and indeed he did not wholly hear; all his senses contracted, denying comprehension to the terrible words. He made a conscious effort after that to do whatever he could to make it easier for the rest of them, short of the impossible effort of ceasing to drink.

When he was out he did his very best not to come home until after the children were in bed, a difficult thing for him to do, for there always occurred a stage, impossible to schedule in advance, when the urge to be in Bea's presence became far too insistent to control.

But I wasn't hurting them, I *wasn't*. Even on the nights when he had been unable to stay away until after the children were in bed, they seldom noticed anything. And if they did, he swept them, like bug-eyed elves, into an enchanted realm of forgetfulness where the only tears were of delight.

"Aha!" he'd cry when he came, bearing himself with the most exquisite steadiness, into the tiny kitchen, "Aha, I see the audience is assembled." Then with practiced discretion he would cross the room, walking an inch or so from the wall, brushing the wall for support with his elbow and the tips of his fingers, and sit down quite upright in a chair beside the kitchen table.

"Property man?" he'd command benignly, and Harold would scurry to the buffet and bring the white shoe box in which they kept the disappearing penny, the magic handkerchief, the flying pencil, and the talking playing cards. The children would seat themselves across the table and the performance would begin.

Bea, he knew, had some conception of the terrible concentration and effort it took to make his thick fingers and his wavering eyes do his bidding. But, in that whole last year, he never failed them once. There were false starts and temporary disasters, but always in the long run the disappearing penny did disappear, the magic handkerchief did change its shape and color under their very eyes, and the flying pencil did travel, unseen, from an inner pocket to an outer ear and the talking playing cards did reveal their identities; and the whole room glowed with their wonder and respect.

"Show me how! Just show me the card trick," Harold would beg whispering, as though in the presence of a king.

"Someday," Chris would promise warmly. "When you get a little older, I'll show you."

"Will I really be able to do it?"

"Someday you'll be able to do it, Harold."

"But, gee"—Harold's tone hung between skepticism and reckless exultation—"most *big* people can't even do magic."

"That's because they haven't got somebody to teach them," his father would reassure him. "You'll be able to do it when I teach you."

"Cross your heart?"

"Cross my heart." *Hurt* them!

Harold was six and Kally was five when the parting came. Chris scarcely realized what was happening until it was over. He had been sick, very sick, a searing, tumultuous, two-day ordeal with delirium tremens and then almost a week of lying spent and lifeless on the bed in the back room while Bea fed him soups and horrible honey-sweetened tea. Then, one winter morning, the children came into the room where he lay. They were heavily bundled up as though for sleighing, and they walked up to him with white, scared faces and bent over and kissed him and stole away.

Bea came into the room and sat on the side of the bed. She was hatless, but she wore her galoshes and the thick overcoat that she had bought in a secondhand store and made over and dyed with a package of ten-cent dye that had not worked quite as well as expected.

"We're going now, Chris dear," she said softly.

"Going?" Chris said. "Going?" He tried to sit up, but he was not yet equal to the effort.

"Mrs. Brown downstairs will look in for the next few days. There's stuff in the icebox."

"What do you mean, going?" Chris cried wildly. But he saw the futility and injustice of argument and he lay back, trembling silently.

Bea lay down on the bed beside him and turned her face to his. It was no longer a young face, but it still had its quiet, steady strength. She reached for his thin shoulders and drew him across to her, resting him against her firm warm body. She held him like that, utterly soundless, for a long time, perhaps a full minute, perhaps ten minutes, perhaps an hour. He felt himself relaxing. He closed his eyes, either asleep or pretending to be asleep, he never was quite sure when he tried to remember. At last she put her lips very close to his ear and whispered quietly: "I love you, Chris. We all love you and we know you love us." And then she carefully removed her arms from his shoulders and tiptoed away.

The light on the kitchen ceiling fluttered helplessly. The gasoline motor outside delivered itself of a resentful death rattle and Chris was suddenly alone in the room with the hostile moonlight.

"Roxy!" he shouted fearfully. "Roxy, wake up! The light's gone out."

He scrambled around the table and shook Brannick's shoulder, but Brannick remained as imperturbably inanimate as a sack of cement. He felt his way back, touching the wall as he went, to the far corner of the room, to where the black shadow of a box telephone brooded above the black bulk of the wood box.

He took the receiver in one hand and pawed at the handle of the mechanism with his other hand and began turning it furiously. It was a long time before he got an answer.

"That you, Miss Shaw?" he shouted. "Long distance. I want to talk to Mrs. Sondern in Elevator."

"Who's that, Mr. Sondern or Mr. Brannick?" The voice at the other end was cold and unfriendly as the moon itself. "Do you realize it's after midnight?"

"You never mind that, Miss Shaw," Chris shouted, his voice loud but clear. "You better just put that call through."

"Very well, if you *insist*. What's the number in Elevator, please?"

"You never mind that, Miss Shaw," Chris shouted. "You just ask the operator in Elevator for Mrs. Sondern. She'll know all right."

And after a time, a very long time, of course, but still in time, her friendly anxious voice came to him from out of the pale, menacing moonlight.

"Hello, Chris."

"Hello, Bea.

"I'm sorry I got you up, Bea."

"That's all right, Chris."

"I just wanted to say hello."

"That was nice, Chris."

"I'm sorry about coming to Dobie. I don't know how I did it. I didn't mean to do it."

"That's all right, Chris."

"There's nothing to worry about, Bea. I'll never do it again. I won't come to Elevator or anything like that."

"It wouldn't be a good thing, Chris."

"I know, Bea. That's what I wanted to tell you."

"The children are fine, Chris. They're just fine."

"I'm glad to hear that. Well, good-by Bea."

"Good-by, Chris."

He hung up the receiver and felt his way back along the wall to his chair by the kitchen table.

Chapter Nine

After the ball game that Friday night Harold was hanging around the home team's bench when Dutch Reiseling looked up from the water bucket, yelled "Here y'are!" tossed him his pitcher's glove and then bent down again to remove his spikes. It would not have occurred to Harold to ask or even to hope for permission to carry Dutch Reiseling's glove and shoes back to the hotel for him. Normally the honor would already have been spoken for by Rouge the Red Taylor or Charlie Johnson or some other, bolder boy, but something about the way Dutch Reiseling had looked when he came back to the bench had warned all the boys waiting to slap his shoulders or touch his arm that he was not yet ready to select his bearer for this evening.

Dutch had come to bat in the last half of the ninth inning with two out and the bases full and Weyburn ahead of Elevator 6 to 4. Nobody doubted for an instant that Dutch was about to win the ball game, for although Dutch had never come to bat before in such a poetic situation during his brief stay in Elevator, that was largely because Dutch had seldom allowed the outcome of any game to remain in serious doubt so long. The only real question now was whether the ball he hit would clear the crescent of parked automobiles ringing the outfield on the fly or on the bounce. If he did it on the bounce, it would be a ground-rules double and the score would be merely tied; if he did it on the fly, it would be a home run and the game would be over. Each of the three enemy outfielders backed up until his knees were against the bumper of an automobile. The infielders scurried nervously to the brown edges of prairie grass beyond the trampled base lines.

The Weyburn pitcher had a deplorably ineffectual slow ball—such a palpable cripple that no one not bent on suicide would have dared throw it to a hitter like Dutch Reiseling. The Weyburn pitcher threw three slow balls in a row. Dutch let one go by for a ball, pulled the second three hundred feet toward left field and a hundred feet outside the foul line, and missed the third so mightily that he spun right around and almost fell down.

One and two. The Weyburn outfielders pressed their rumps into the chrome grillwork of the encircling automobiles and shrilled thin bleats of fright and supplication to their pitcher. The Weyburn infielders retreated another step or two into the prairie grass. "The old jinniker, Harry!" they cried, in the dismal accents of souls in hell. Dutch Reiseling clenched his teeth and wiped the sweat from his eyes with the sleeve of his long woolen underwear.

The slow ball floated up again. Dutch Reiseling slid his hands down the handle of the bat, crunched over the plate —and bunted! Bunted against every law in the book, against every rule of strategy or sense. Bunted where a double was needed to tie the game or a triple to win. Bunted with a bad hitter coming up behind him. Bunted with two strikes on him and a foul meaning an automatic out. Bunted perfectly down the third base line, bawled "Get moving!" to the three base runners momentarily paralyzed by their as-

tonishment, and raced toward first, while the Weyburn in-
field awoke to hopelessness and horror, like a Doré drawing
come to life.

The Weyburn third baseman was a fat, short man, already going on for elderly. He stood transfixed while the ball
rolled obscenely toward his station. One run had been scored
before he moved. Then, with terror and damnation written
in every line of his quivering face, he began moving his short
fat legs in the direction of the ball. The ball was barely moving when he reached it, but it trickled through his fingers
and he turned and waddled after it again. Now it had
stopped rolling altogether, but the footsteps of another base
runner thundering past might have added to his difficulties,
for he dropped the ball, even in the act of picking it up, and
had to stoop for it a third time. Everyone in the park was
yelling at him; the Elevator rooters in jubilation and scorn,
his own teammates in hatred and despair. By the time he
straightened up with the ball secured in his pudgy fist, he
was bereft of the final trace of dignity and manhood. Two
runs had scored and another was going past third base. The
fat third baseman took careful aim for the plate and threw
the ball into the grandstand. Everybody scored, including
Dutch Reiseling.

"Well, let's get going," Dutch Reiseling said to Harold,
after the press of his admirers had begun to disperse. Since
their first meeting outside the Chinaman's, Dutch had allowed Harold to play catch with him three different times,
but Harold had found it impossible to exult in his good fortune without reservation. He had an uneasy feeling that
Dutch's acceptance of him must have had something to do
with mistaken identity. If Dutch had acted as though he
were sorry for him, Harold would have been grateful but not
mystified. But it did not seem that way at all. Dutch not only
treated Harold as a near equal but as a near equal who had
things to give as well as to receive. After their second work-

out together Harold had mumbled, "Thanks, Dutch." And Dutch had said easily and gravely, and definitely not in the tone of a man making a ridiculous joke: "Okay, kid. Maybe someday you can do something for me."

Dutch couldn't have been thinking of such a thing as allowing Harold to carry his glove and spikes down the main street, in plain view of half the town. That wasn't Harold doing something for him; it was him doing something for Harold. Harold stopped trying to think about it and trudged along happily at Dutch Reiseling's side.

"That boy of theirs in left field—" Dutch addressed Harold not in the tones of a superior lecturing an inferior but as a peer setting forth for the record something already known to both—"that left fielder of theirs. You saw how I got him in the first inning on the changeup. Got him on the changeup again in the fourth. I thought I owned him. Then in the seventh I blew two fast ones past him and wasted two to the corner. He never moved a muscle. Barney called for another fast one. But no, I got him twice before on the changeup and I just had to do it again. Smart. The minute I let it go I knew he'd been waiting for it since the fourth inning. That's why he hadn't moved. He'd made up his mind I could strike him out again on a fast ball or a hook or a slider, but I wasn't striking him out again on a changeup. So he had his timing set for the changeup and he kept it set until the changeup came. The minute I let that big fat grapefruit float out of my hand his face lit up like a kid at Christmas. If there'd been time I'd have turned around and yelled to the outfield to start running. And when I saw her going out of sight I suddenly remembered a thing a man told me back in Regina. He told me: 'A left-hander should never try to think until it's absolutely necessary, and even then he should expect the worst.'"

"Aw, he was lucky," Harold said.

They loafed on down the wooden Main Street sidewalk,

its gray old boards lightly rouged by the final remnants of a summer sunset.

"Tell me, Harold," Dutch said abruptly, "that girl that lives at your place—what's her name?"

"My sister Kally?" Harold said doubtfully. "Her real name's Kathleen."

"No. The other one," Dutch said.

"Oh. Vanny Chatsworth." Harold heard with the very tiniest sense of loss and an engulfment of comfort. He should have known all along that his happy intimacy with Dutch Reiseling had some connection with Dutch Reiseling's intention to Fix Vanny Chatsworth Up. The knowledge now carried far more relief than disillusionment. He felt no disappointment at having been deceived, for he had been expecting to learn of some far more callous deception. He could not think of a finer thing to do than to help his friend Dutch Reiseling Fix his friend Vanny Chatsworth Up. He had always felt a little sad that Vanny wasn't able to skate and dance and swim on account of her delicate health. From Dutch Reiseling's confident tone and his benign expression on the day when Harold had heard him discussing Vanny across the street by the Chinaman's, Harold had no doubt whatever of his ability to restore Vanny to full robustness. How the therapy was to be performed Harold had no idea. But Dutch Reiseling was not a man who lied and he was not a man who overestimated his powers. And Dutch had said quite plainly that after he got through Vanny would go marching down the street like somebody leading a parade. If Dutch said it would be that way, that's the way it would be. And Harold was proud to be included in the enterprise, even though some prudent instinct told him it would be best to pretend that he did not even know the enterprise existed. Dutch, he remembered, had spoken of it in a lowered voice. For some reason he seemed to want it kept a secret.

Between persons of genuine sensitivity, a difference of age is quite inconsequential. Even though he had the wit to recognize the need for secrecy in one particular, Harold might easily have blundered into direct speech in another. He might have said now to Dutch Reiseling, "On warm evenings, Vanny always sits out on the front porch, reading. Would you like to come and sit on the front porch for a while with me?"

Instead Harold, being a sensitive person, said: "Say, Dutch, did you ever take the Earl Leiderman body-building course?"

"No," Dutch said, "but I bet it's a waste of time."

"I sent in a coupon. They keep sending me literature and bringing the price down. I don't know whether I should take it or not."

"Uh-huh," Dutch said absently. He was looking ahead along the street.

Harold was glad the last light was now almost gone, for his sense of brazenness and dissembling was written in crimson across his face—"You couldn't take a minute to come up and see the stuff the Earl Leiderman people put out, could you?"

"Well——" For the last twenty or thirty seconds they had been in full view of the Chatsworth residence. A slender figure in a white organdy dress could be seen quite clearly against the dark vines trailing toward the far end of the veranda. "Why not?" Dutch Reiseling said.

As they turned into the yard and mounted the few steps to the veranda, Vanny raised her eyes and then returned quickly to her book. "Hello, Vanny," Harold said.

"Hello, Harold." Vanny's reply was pleasant enough but she did not look up from her book.

"This is Dutch Reiseling." Dutch had removed his baseball cap. "I mean Mr. Dutch Reiseling," Harold corrected himself quickly.

Vanny nodded timidly and fled back into her book.

"He bunted with the bases full," Harold boasted. "The bases were full and two out and we were two behind. He bunted in four runs."

"That's nice," Vanny acknowledged feebly. She darted a frightened glance to the door leading into the house, but perceived that Dutch Reiseling stood between it and her, regarding her with silent good will. Dutch Reiseling moved a step closer. Harold wished that Vanny would look straight up at him so that she might see the kind and noblehearted way in which he was smiling at her. He wondered if that smile alone might not be enough to accomplish the splendid task afoot.

Harold went and put his hand on the door but he did not open it. He perceived that in the face of Vanny's embarrassment, Dutch's customary confidence had shown a small tendency to desertion. Dutch was fidgeting with his cap. Suddenly he took two steps and sat down on the porch davenport at Vanny's side. For a moment neither of them said anything and then each blurted a remark in the same instant.

"I hear you're a pitcher," Vanny declared primly.

"I see you're reading," Dutch Reiseling announced.

Vanny now seemed to shrink a little. Quite obviously her courage and her social resources had been almost exhausted by the one remark. But as though he saw that he was not really being spurned but only fled from, Dutch became more confident and easy. He reached over gently and took the open book she had been reading from Vanny's hands.

The light was now almost gone and he had to hold the book close to his face to read from it. Vanny turned her head toward him cautiously. A gust of breeze brushed past the ivy and mingled the strong, sweaty, slightly sour masculine smell of Dutch Reiseling's stained uniform with the tiny, almost forlorn fragrance of Vanny Chatsworth.

Dutch leafed through a few pages and began to read almost at once. His momentary uncertainty and self-consciousness were gone and he read gaily and confidently like the cocky troubadour beside the Chinaman's billboard—not quite teasing, not altogether bragging, neither apologizing nor demanding, not quite inviting or insisting, just saying a big and pleasant thing that anybody could listen to or not or make as much of or as little as they chose. Harold kept his hand on the doorknob and his eyes glued on Vanny's face; he would not have been surprised to see the metamorphosis and cure begin to happen in this very instant.

" 'The fountains mingle with the river,' "
Dutch was reading,

" 'And the rivers with the ocean,
The winds of heaven mix for ever with a sweet emotion.' "

"That's Shelley," Vanny said quickly. "Do you like pitching?"

"Sure, but I'd rather hit.
'Nothing in the world is single:
All things by a law divine
In one another's being mingle——' "

"It was nice that you won tonight," Vanny cut in again. "What was the score?"

"Eight-six. 'Why not I with thine?' "

Dutch smiled gravely at Vanny through the gloom to reassure her that there was no need for anyone to take anything personally.

" 'See the mountains kiss high heaven
And the waves clasp one another;
No sister flower would be forgiven
If it disdained its brother.' "

Vanny had shrunk away to the far corner of the chesterfield. Dutch made no attempt to move closer to her, and his voice became a trace more distant. But it was still full of kindness.

"'And the sunlight clasps the earth
And the moonbeams kiss the sea—
What are all these kissings worth,
If thou kiss not me?' P. B. Shelley.

"Is that supposed to be good?" he asked her with disarming matter-of-factness.

"Oh," Vanny said intensely, "he couldn't have written anything bad."

Dutch Reiseling straightened himself on the davenport. The slight movement suggested he had really come on important business. "You're the librarian here, aren't you?"

"Yes."

"I read all the time. I'd rather read than anything—even play ball."

Vanny did not say anything.

"I mean magazines and papers and things like that," Dutch said quickly, a little like someone caught out in something close to a lie. "I buy every magazine that comes into the drugstore and every Sunday paper too. I read every word. I just can't stand not to have something to read." He paused a minute. "You ask Mr. Brown down at the drugstore sometime."

Vanny clearly did not know how to treat this surge of information. She smoothed her white organdy dress down past her smooth slender knees and cast a bleak, helpless smile at Harold through the gathering night.

"I only found out the other day they have a library here. I guess I could join, couldn't I?"

"Anybody can join," Vanny said primly. "I mean anyone is welcome to join," she amended.

"I'll come and see you then," Dutch said. "Why don't you come and see me play ball sometime? I could have had a tryout with Minneapolis once."

Harold felt the doorknob in his hand turning. Through the open screen the lean and hostile visage of Vanny Chatsworth's mother fixed them all, distantly and forbiddingly. "Vanny!" Vanny rose at once, stumbling in her haste and confusion. "It's time you were in bed, Vanny; you know this night air's the worst thing in the world for you."

"How do——" Dutch Reiseling was on his feet beginning to bow, beginning to walk a step toward Vanny's mother, beginning to hold out his hand. But the door was open and Vanny was inside and the door was closed again and Harold and Dutch were alone on the veranda and everything was in almost total darkness.

"Well," Dutch said, putting his hand on Harold's shoulder and giving him a tiny, high-spirited squeeze, "that's the way it goes. Let's go and have a look at that stuff from Earl Leiderman."

Harold's mother made them cocoa and Dutch turned out to know several of the hymns that they knew. Looking back on it, Harold was reasonably confident that even if the first part of the evening might have been a disappointment for Dutch, the cocoa and all might have made up for it.

Chapter Ten

Amelia Chatsworth never had a chance. There was no certain way to protect her daughter Vanessa from Dutch Reiseling.

Dutch could not get Vanny off his mind. His urge to be with her and partake of her was not in immediate need of satisfying, but her mere presence in the universe on her mother's grudging terms left him with a nagged and taunted feeling. He made no attempt to define his thoughts, but the fact that a fine, firm girl like Vanny could be so withdrawn and lonely struck him as an affront to the entire human race. There was something desperately wrong with a world in which Vanny Chatsworth sat by herself on porches and in libraries reeking of last week's furniture polish while Dutch Reiseling walked by himself through empty streets.

Dutch joined the library. The first evening he went there Vanny told him she was sorry but he would not be able to take out any books. He needed two character references and it was necessary for them to put their names in writing on a form. Vanny said she was sorry but those were the rules. Dutch said he understood. That was on a Monday night.

On the Wednesday he was back with his character references and ten cents for a library card. By now, although
Vanny did not know it, he knew Vanny very well. He knew
her on moonlit hillsides and he knew her in the rustle of
fallen leaves at the edge of poplar bluffs. He knew her where
and how he would meet her soon, where and how he had
met other good, deserving friends. He knew her in soft grass
beside the slow river at the bottom of the valley. He knew
her well enough to go directly to a book of poems called
The Golden Treasury and ask her to help him understand
it. He leaned across the wide table in the deserted room and
said to her:

"'Much have I travelled in the realms of gold
And many goodly states and kingdoms seen;
Round many western islands have I been
Which bards in fealty to Apollo hold.'

"I don't get that fealty to Apollo."

"He was the god of the sun," Vanny informed him
dutifully.

"Sure, sure; but what about that fealty?"

"I think it means the poets think they're islands of the
sun."

"Oh," Dutch said. "Say, here's a good one." He read to
her in a calm and confident voice. "It's called advice to a
girl:

"'Men when their affairs require
Must a while themselves retire;
Sometimes hunt, sometimes hawk,
And not ever sit and talk.
If these and such like you can bear
Then like and love and never fear.'

"Some poetry! Bear is supposed to rhyme with fear."

"Well"—Vanny bridled slightly as though her personal responsibility as librarian were being called into question—
"rhyming isn't everything."

Dutch Reiseling knew her on the perfumed edges of August wheat fields and in ravines full of the whisper of melting snow.

"I'm sorry," Vanny said, "but I have to close up now. Have you decided what you want to take?"

"Yes," he said. "I'll take the book of poems. Would you like me to walk home with you?"

"No thank you," Vanny said.

He knew her under stars and faint street lamps. He knew her footsteps on gray wooden sidewalks and he knew her arm under his own firm hand, stiff and terrified of the patient certainty waiting there. When they reached her door, he drew his arm away. "Good night," he said courteously. "Good night," Vanny said, trying without success to hide her terror. "I'll see you again," Dutch said gently.

Amelia never had a chance.

Harold felt he had a stake and proper interest in what might happen between Dutch Reiseling and Vanny Chatsworth. By oblique inquiry he had learned that the slanting man had left Elevator forever and there was little chance of any bet being collected or paid between him and Dutch. The question, therefore, of Dutch's benefactions toward Vanny had become philosophical rather than financial. But Harold's interest did not wane, for he was a friend of both of them. On the summer nights he left his window open. The window overlooked the veranda. He was working on a cartooning course that had come to him at a nominal charge from a famous cartooning firm in Chicago. In the early times of his investigation, Vanny always arrived home on library nights at four minutes after ten. These times were slowly extended to six minutes after ten and then to eight minutes after ten and then as late as eleven minutes after ten. By then Harold could almost tell the minute of Vanny's arrival by the number of times that Mrs. Chatsworth had opened the door below, walked to the edge of the veranda, and turned back inside.

Harold, of course, was in a better position than Mrs. Chatsworth to know why Vanny was late. From his upper room he could see through the intervening thicket of caragana hedge and Manitoba maple to the corner where Vanny and Dutch Reiseling parted. He had no sense at all of spying on them. He was glad to notice that they did not stoop to the ridiculous and demeaning activity he had been taught to describe as "smooching." They parted cleanly, with hurried, quiet words. Vanny rushed into sight of her home and Dutch sauntered back downtown toward the Chinaman's. Some nights Vanny's mother opened the door before Vanny reached it.

"You're late!"

"Not very, Mother," Vanny would say.

"Try to be on time. I worry so much."

"Yes, Mother."

One night Vanny was very, very late. Harold sat upstairs and Mrs. Chatsworth sat downstairs waiting and watching until away past midnight. Harold would have gone to bed, but at just past a quarter after ten Mrs. Chatsworth began talking in a loud and not quite understandable way to Mr. Chatsworth. At a quarter to eleven she telephoned the town constable and at a quarter past eleven she telephoned the reeve and demanded that he form a search party. So Harold did not feel he could go to bed. At a quarter past twelve Vanny marched up the street alone. Harold's eyes were almost drugged with the need of sleep, but in the distance he had seen a shadowy figure move away from her side at the end of the block. Vanny's mother was at the gate, clenching it with stiffened hands. Mr. Chatsworth stood on the porch. The lights from the porch and the lit-up parlor, intensified as they bounced back from the dark maple trees at the edges of the yard, threw them all into bright relief, like actors on a stage.

"Vanessa!" Her mother sobbed and pushed her gray and ropy hair back from her eyes.

"Vanessa! Where have you been? Where in the Name of our Loving Father have you been?"

Vanny's face was as set as marble as Harold peered down through the screen of his window. "Vanessa, for God's sake! Where have you been?" Mrs. Chatsworth sobbed. Vanny touched her mother gently on the arm.

"I was detained," Vanny announced in tones of wonder and went quietly through the door.

The next day was a Saturday and Harold spied on her when she left the house to go to the library. She held her breasts and shoulders high and her steps went quickly up and down as though every separate silence and click of her heels was an alternating act of flight from and union with the world. Harold knew what Dutch Reiseling had meant when he had promised that Vanny would sometime walk like the leader of a parade.

Chapter Eleven

"You know," Mrs. Sondern said, "I think I'll make something for the fair." She beamed on her children with gracious and moderately patronizing good will.

Kally emitted a satisfying gurgle of excitement, and even Harold, whose fine edge of enthusiasm for his mother's creative projects had been somewhat dulled by time, managed a brave if insincere "Oh boy!"

"Gee, Mother," Kally said, "I'll bet anything you win a ribbon. What you going to make?"

"Well, now, let's see. Let's see."

"Make a doily, Mother," Kally said. "Make a nice lace doily."

Harold felt things closing in on him and suffocating him, like the water when you jumped off the dam and forgot to hold your nose. It was just like fighting for breath while he watched the long flicker of indecision march across his mother's face.

"I don't think so." To Harold the words boomed forth like a message of reprieve. "I never made many doilies, Kally. Anyway, there isn't time."

"There's two days," Kally said. "I bet you could make a doily in two days. Or maybe a nice embroidered runner."

Harold was fighting for his breath again. He'd never known Kally to be so stupid.

"Make something to eat!" Harold meant it to sound airy and light, just an offhand suggestion, but the panic in his chest swirled up into his throat and left his voice halfway between a bleat and a croak.

His mother looked at him in astonishment. "My goodness, boy, you got an awful frog. You're not catching cold are you?"

"A pie!" Kally yelled. "A great big punkin pie."

Harold could have strangled her. His mother's pumpkin pies were wonderful to eat, but even the idiot fancy of a girl oughtn't to have misjudged their scenic properties, which were unconventional to say the least. In Mrs. Sondern's hot oven their fillings crusted and then burst into deep crevices, like drying lava.

"I know," Harold said with remarkable calm. "Bread. Make a loaf of bread."

"Bread!" Kally sniffed. "Anybody can make bread."

That, in substance, was Harold's very point, although he wouldn't have put it so tactlessly.

"Yeah?" he said. "But anybody can't win a prize for making bread. Nobody ever wins the blue ribbon for bread but Mrs. Lillington."

"Umm. That's right," Mrs. Sondern conceded thoughtfully. "Seems to me I remember them talking down at Morganson's one day about Mrs. Lillington's bread."

At the mention of Mrs. Lillington Kally's eyes had lighted evilly. "That stuck-up old thing?" Kally said vindictively. "On second thought I second the motion. Make bread."

Once Harold's idea was accepted, Mrs. Sondern and Kally set about dramatizing it with all their customary enthusiasm for any new scheme, building it up and embellishing it, and investing it with an importance far beyond the limits of safe restraint. They agreed that, after all, making bread was one of the basic accomplishments of the human race. Indeed, what accomplishment was more deserving of respect? No wonder Mrs. Lillington had achieved so durable a celebrity through her ability to make the best bread in a dozen townships. And if Mrs. Lillington was famous, how much more famous would her ultimate conqueror be?

"Gee, Ma," Kally sighed, suddenly awed by the magnitude of the undertaking. "There's no telling where it might lead. I bet if you win you could start selling bread."

"Well now, that's not such a foolish idea at that," Mrs. Sondern agreed. "I'll bet old Morganson sells at least a hundred loaves of his old train bread every week. A hundred times nine cents, that's—why—imagine that—it's ninety dollars!"

"Nine dollars," Harold grumped.

"Nine—why it can't be, Harold," Mrs. Sondern said reasonably. "He must sell far more than nine dollars' worth of bread a week."

"A hundred times nine cents is nine dollars," Harold said stubbornly.

"Well then," Mrs. Sondern said, in the patient, sympathetic tone of an experienced debater who has caught an opponent in an error of spectacular fatuity, and is too kind to rub it in. "Well then, Mr. Morganson must sell five hundred loaves a week. How much is that?"

Kally glared triumphantly at her brother. "Smarty!" she said.

Kally scarcely slept at all that night. Or at least so she said, and there was no denying that she *was* excited. But Harold was quite unprepared for the staggering indiscretions into which her blind enthusiasm led her the next day.

Walking home from school at noon, a couple of his class-

mates caught up with him. Kally was walking a little further behind with some girls.

"Hear your mother's going in the fair," one of the boys
said. He said it good-naturedly enough, but still in a banter-
ing kind of way and Harold felt his face going red.

"Oh," Harold mumbled, doing his best to make it sound
completely unimportant. "News to me."

"I hear she's putting in some bread."

"Bread," Harold said reflectively. "I didn't know they had
bread in the fair. I thought it was only horses and pigs and
stuff. In Regina that's all they had. They had a midway too.
Great big merry-go-rounds and Ferris wheels and side shows.
One time . . ."

Another boy interrupted rudely: "Oh no, you didn't
know. Not much you didn't know."

The two boys stopped to let the girls behind them catch
up. Harold stopped too, but didn't turn around. He heard
one of the boys yell, "Hey, Kally—Kally Sondern! Your
bread still gonna beat old lady Lillington?"

Kally's voice was a little shrill but unabashed. "You
heard me the first time," she acknowledged.

Another girl's voice giggled: "She bets a thousand dollars."

"Hah!" Kally yelled. "That's all *you* know. I bet a *million*
dollars."

This provoked a burst of hoots. Over his shoulder Harold
urged, "Come on Kally, we got to hurry on home. We
haven't got much time."

"I bet *two* million dollars," Kally was saying belligerently.
"I bet a billion billion quadrillion dollars."

Harold dragged her away by the arm. "Shut up," he
hissed. "Shut up." She tugged away from him and shouted
over her shoulder: "You know what? My ma's bread always
used to win the ribbon at the *Regina* fair."

They walked home in silence. There was nothing he

could tell her, there was no use trying to tell her—she just wouldn't learn anything except by learning it herself. From the depths of his misery and foreboding, Harold dredged up just one plaintive reproach: "Gee whiz, Kally, gee whiz."

But the iron had driven into his soul. He would have nothing to do with it now, neither with the bread nor with the fair itself. If his mother would only get sick, he thought— not real sick, but just sick enough that she couldn't bake in the morning—or if the stovepipes would clog up as they sometimes did, or—— Harold didn't sleep much that night either.

He was up at dawn, though, helping to get the fire going, and he was kind and strangely tender toward them both, as though the least he could offer them was this sad substitute for his confidence. When his mother was nearly finished kneading the dough Harold asked: "Can I butter the pan for you, Ma?" And when they opened the oven door and his mother held aloft the white-and-silver embryo of dough and brand-new tin for a moment of dedication, her face shiny with heat and satisfaction, and cried "Well, here goes!"—then Harold cried "Well, here goes!" too, and with an even greater appearance of heartiness than Kally's second echo.

After their early breakfast, Harold went out and sat in the yard pinking marbles up against the side of the house for practice. Kally came out and sat down beside him after a while. Her face was curiously strained and she didn't say much. She was scared, Harold saw, maybe for the first time in her life. He took her hand and began pulling on the ends of her fingers, one by one, to see how many of the knuckles would crack, a game they had. Only one of them cracked. "One boy friend," Harold said. "Who is it?"

They usually joked about it, but now Kally just looked at him gratefully and answered quietly, without smiling: "You, Harold."

They sat back with their shoulders against the side of the house and their faces into the sun, their eyes nearly closed and their hands still touching, savoring the uncomplicated comfortableness of being all alone together in the yard, with their mother nearby, alone in the kitchen. "You're not really going to stay home from the fair are you Harold?" Kally pleaded. "No," he answered, surrendering to a quiet gust of pity. "I guess I might as well go for a while."

"Harold."

"Uh-huh."

"I'm sorry I bragged so much to the other kids."

"Aw, why shouldn't you brag?" Harold said. His words astonished him.

They sat on in the sun. At last their mother opened the upstairs window very quietly and whispered out to them: "Just about done. Want to see it come out?"

They tiptoed upstairs and Harold fitted the stairway door back into place as carefully as though it were a piece of fine bric-a-brac. Then they tiptoed into the kitchen. Their mother took a dishcloth in her hand and lowered the oven door by inches until it had come to full rest on its hinges. Then very slowly, using both hands, she lifted the pan of bread out of the oven, backed carefully across the room and placed it on a double sheet of newspaper on the table. Harold could hardly bear to look, but when he did he had to fight back a shout of astonishment and relief. The bread bulged out magnificently from the seared tin, bronzed and rounded and satiny, like a giant's bicep. It was a magnificent and totally unprecedented sight, and it made him feel all weak and weepy. "Gosh, Ma," he said huskily. "Gosh, Ma."

"Smell it too!" Kally breathed exultantly.

"Gosh, Ma," Harold whispered. "What did you *do?*"

Their mother's chuckle had the amiable, tipsy arrogance of the chuckle of a drunk who has just discovered that he is capable of flying like a bird. "It *is* pretty good, isn't it?"

"Pretty good!"

"Of course," their mother explained patronizingly, if a little uncertainly, "when you're baking for a fair you're a little more careful about your oven and your basting and things."

"It's not so—kind of white and crackly," Harold observed, still bewildered.

"No," Mrs. Sondern concurred. "When you're baking for a fair you want it brown and sort of smooth."

They stood and looked at the bread for fully five minutes, whispering over it, their voices as soft and vibrant as the bread's own pulsing fragrance. At last their mother said, more briskly: "Suppose you make up the entry paper, Harold, while Kally and I get dressed."

Before they were halfway to the fairgrounds Harold's spirits had begun to sink again, or rather to temporize and calculate and issue mean little warnings that gradually destroyed the dizzy lifted feeling he'd had a while before. He was between the other two as they walked arm in arm up the Main Street sidewalk to the top end of the town, and as he glanced at their faces he saw that both of them were eager and unafraid, if a little nervous. His own assurance nearly returned, but when they passed the school turn, he remembered there'd be school again on Monday, with everybody talking about the fair and paying homage to those who had earned new distinction and exacting penalties from those who had earned new shame. Abruptly all the things from which the other two drew excitement became, to him, fresh sources of uneasiness. The loaded cars loafing past them, with an occasional horse-drawn Democrat sandwiched in between, seemed suddenly to have a single dynamic. The haughty high-stepping percheron stallion that minced up the street behind a jogging buggy, leering suggestively to either side; the town band braying in the distance; the three-colored muslin banner above the gate that read: "Elevator Agricultural Society 38th Annual Fair;

Come One Come All"; the swirl and chatter and the still tentative barnyard smells inside the gate which betokened that the fair had not yet fully settled down for the long day ahead—these were all part of a dismaying conspiracy, a conspiracy to assemble the whole world in witness to the absurd, doomed, affronting challenge of Mrs. Sondern, B.

"There's sure a lot of people," Harold observed abjectly.

"Umm." His mother closed her change purse and handed each of them a ticket.

Inside the gate Harold said quickly, "Well, so long. See you later."

"Don't you want to come with us while Ma puts the bread in?" Kally asked, disappointed.

"I'll find it later," Harold muttered.

"I think they judge the bread at three." Mrs. Sondern eyed the brown-paper parcel in her arm and looked around to see if any of the people standing near the gate had noticed she'd brought something to enter.

Harold started to disappear into the crowd. Then Kally was beside him, yelling with uncalled-for vehemence: "The entry! You forgot to give us the entry slip."

"Keep your shirt on!" Harold whispered savagely. He fumbled inside his cotton jersey and thrust the plain envelope at her quickly.

"Have you still got your two dimes?" Kally asked him. Two or three farmers had stopped and were looking at them. Harold started to walk away again. "Ma says not more than one ice-cream cone. You're to eat something substantial, a hot dog or something."

Harold had reached the corner of a small refreshment booth. He slipped around its corner and disappeared gratefully into a noisy maze of hogpens and cattle runs, an oasis of forgetfulness where the striving was abstract and unfelt, and nothing had anything to do with him.

He didn't see Kally again for a long time, until away after

half past two. He knew the time approximately because a man he'd asked, over near the cattle-judging ring, had told him it was two a long time earlier. It was after that that Harold had started to watch the ball game, from away out past center field, lying down between two parked cars, almost right underneath one of them. From this position he couldn't see all of the ball diamond, but he could see most of it. He told himself he wasn't hiding. Why should he hide? It was comfortable, that was all, and when somebody got a long hit you could really see better here than anywhere. He'd just watch a couple more innings, and then he'd get up and go over to the bakery building and he'd still be in plenty of time for the judging. It wouldn't be right to miss that unless he happened to miss it by accident. His mother would think he didn't care if he wasn't there to see the judging. He wasn't going to miss it. It was a good ball game, that was all. Elevator wasn't playing in this game and therefore his friend Dutch Reiseling wasn't playing either. But it was still a good ball game to watch.

Kally's voice was right in his ear, as loud and frantic as a sudden burst from the automobile horn above him. "Harold! Where have you *been?*"

His guilty start carried him all the way to his feet. His eyes barely brushed her face before they fell, but he saw that she was nearly crying with exasperation and relief.

"Come on, it's after three already!" Accusation and supplication fought for mastery over her hurrying words.

Harold started off with her, circling behind the line of cars around the outfield. "I thought there was lots of time," he mumbled.

"They were just getting ready to start the judging when I left," Kally nagged. "I've been looking all over for you."

He quickened his pace reluctantly as she pulled at his sleeve, fighting through the goalless swarms of people. They bumped into a woman with an armful of bottled preserves and then into a man leading a calf on a rope, and Harold tried halfheartedly to slow Kally to a more dignified pace. But she panted on relentlessly; she didn't even stop to straighten her hair, or wipe the sweat off her face, before she dragged him through a half-open doorway into a high barnlike building away on the other side of the grounds near the gate.

Harold had to blink once or twice before he could see very well. At first it was as gloomy and quiet as the inside of a church, but in a moment he began to pick things out, first the small semicircle of people, mostly kids and women, standing in front of a long wooden table, and then two other women and one man walking slowly along in front of the table, stopping every step or so to peer down at something on the table; then the something they were looking at, a long row of loaves of bread, each loaf naked except for a blank envelope lying in front of it on the table.

Kally pulled him into the semicircle of people and he was beside his mother. "They've just started," Mrs. Sondern whispered very reverently, much lower than a church whisper. "Those are the judges."

Harold recognized only two of the judges, Mrs. Knowles, the minister's wife, a plump lady who always held her chin down and her eyes up, as though she were suppressing a belch, and Mr. Shawncross, the undertaker, also plump but more solemn. The lady he failed to recognize didn't seem to count anyway. She was always a step or two behind the other two and when they paused a little longer than usual to exchange whispers over any loaf of bread that seemed to call for discussion, she was always left out of it.

They seemed to be taking a terribly long time. They made one spasmodic funeral march the full length of the table and then marched back again.

"All they're doing is poking and staring," Kally hissed impatiently. "When are they going to start tasting it?"

"They don't taste it," Mrs. Sondern whispered back. "They can tell by the looks and smell."

"That's crazy! How can they tell if they don't know what it tastes like!" Kally's whisper broke in mid-career and finished as a full-bodied stage aside. Harold winced and their mother went, "Shush!" There was a sound of scuffling and giggling behind them and from the back of the semicircle of spectators, a mocking preadolescent croak: "Bet a trillion. Bet a zillion."

A woman's head floated in from the semi-gloom above a set of impossibly high shoulders and an impossibly long and sinuous neck, and suspended itself just above the level of Harold's eyes, glaring at him with accusing bitterness. "Good afternoon, Mrs. Lillington," Harold tried to whisper, surprised and perturbed to see Mrs. Lillington there at all, but determined to convince her that the unseemly noise was not of any Sondern's making, to convince her, moreover, that the Sonderns neither bore her their enmity nor wished to cultivate hers. Before her frozen stare his words died in a soundless grimace.

Now the judges seemed to be making up their minds. They pushed half a dozen loaves of bread toward the back of the table, peered for a while at the remainder, then pushed back another eight or ten. The waiting had now become as dismal and two-dimensional as the dim shed itself, a dead blob of unreality suspended in a stagnant bath of time. Harold felt desperately cold. He remembered and for the first time understood a line he'd read in a book: "*The greaser broke into a cold sweat as Steve yelled, 'Reach!'*" He put his hand up to his forehead; to his surprise there was no sweat of any kind there.

Now there were only six loaves left in front of the judges. Then three and then two.

Harold's eyes sought frantically to pierce the gloom. But the two objects over which the three judges were hovering had no real identity for him. He did not dare to hope that either could really be his mother's loaf of bread; indeed, he now found himself hoping the opposite, as though by making the opposite true he could change the whole tense of these agonizing moments and transfer them from the present to the more merciful constituency of the past. He deliberately took his eyes away from the two loaves in front of the judges and probed among the loaves they had rejected. These were even less distinct. Nevertheless, he picked one out of the rejected loaves and decided it was undeniably theirs. It was right at the very back and therefore one of the first to have been disqualified from further consideration, one of the sorriest and most vulnerable to ridicule and pity.

"Why don't they taste it?" Kally was whispering with excruciating impatience.

"Shh." In the white faces of her children Mrs. Sondern caught her first real inkling of the dismaying, definitive nature of this undertaking she had regarded up to now as a casual adventure. Her whisper was full of comfort and tenderness, like a lullaby. "Shh. They're going to decide now."

Mr. Shawncross turned and faced the little half moon of spectators, his round face bewildered and anxious.

"I see that some of the—ah—probable contestants are included in our—ah—audience. We were—ah—wondering if it's possible that through a misunderstanding some good lady might have entered—ah—two loaves rather than the—ah—single loaf permitted under the rules." As he finished this little speech, his glance rested for a full second on Mrs. Lillington.

"No?" Worried, he went back into consultation with Mrs. Knowles and the other lady.

Kally leaned toward her mother and hissed a *sotto-voce* diatribe. "I-know-why-he-did-that-and-looked-at-her-like-that. He-knows-one-of-them-is-hers-but-he's-not-sure-which-one-and-he's-afraid-of-giving-the-ribbon-to-the-other-one."

"Shh."

At last the nervous conferring ended. From his coat pocket Mr. Shawncross produced a blue silk ribbon and placed it on the table in front of one of the two loaves under arbitration. Then he produced another blue ribbon and placed it in front of the other loaf.

He turned again and made another little speech. "We find we cannot—ah—differentiate between two examples of —ah—perfection. So, although it is a little—ah—irregular, the judges have decided to—ah—make duplicate awards of the —ah—first prize."

He was looking anxiously again at Mrs. Lillington. Mrs. Lillington stared him down with splendid scorn and Mr. Shawncross shrank back guiltily, and fumbled at the white envelopes inside which lay the secret of the winners' identities. When he opened the first envelope and looked at the little slip inside, he seemed to wilt even more, and he opened the second in pawing, all-thumbs haste. He sighed audibly. His smile when he turned again was still a little sickly, though not quite so helpless.

"One of our—ah—winners will be no—ah—surprise." The resolute cheerfulness with which he turned his foundering beam on Mrs. Lillington was an ornament to human fortitude. "I—ah—refer of course—to—that talented and charming—ah—perennial and nonpareil—Mrs. Eunice Lillington. May the judges, my dear Mrs. Lillington, extend their hearty congratulations on the—ah—successful extension of your long and honorable reign as the queen of the—ah—highest and oldest—ah—most exalted of all the—ah—civilized domestic arts." Mr. Shawncross put a special accent on the word "reign." Mrs. Lillington rewarded him with a baring of her teeth.

"The—ah—other winner is a comparative newcomer in our midst—Mrs. Beatrice Sondern. Our congratulations, Mrs. Sondern."

Kally squealed out loud. The words rocked Harold with physical force and he lurched unsteadily against his mother's side, numb and rubbery with swift exhilaration.

"Gracious," Mrs. Sondern gasped. "Gracious."

People were coming to offer their congratulations, some sincere and kindly, some faintly resentful, some incredulous, but all respectful.

Harold distinctly heard old Mrs. Banks, one of the most critical of all the ladies on the laundry list, tell herself in a stupefied mumble as she moved toward the door: "My goodness, I wouldn't have thought that woman could even boil water right." The remark did not anger him, it seemed somehow to be the crowning tribute of all. As the kids who had been giggling behind them began to disperse, Kally holding her mother's arm possessively shouted after them: "When do I get my zillion dollars?"

One of the kids shouted back: "Aw, she didn't win, she only tied." But there was genuine respect in his voice and a willingness to conciliate.

They did not seem able to bring themselves to go. Soon the three of them were all alone in the big dim building. They moved closer to the table and looked wonderingly on the two fine loaves of bread; it was easy to see why it had been so hard for the judges, for the two loaves looked like twins, almost identical in size and shape and in their rounded brownness. "Ours is the best," Kally said giddily, not really caring.

"You bet," Harold said, not really caring either. He snuggled his head up against his mother's side and felt her arm coming around his shoulders, as firm and solid as it used to feel when he was only three or four. Outside the band was playing "Colonel Bogey" and a great shout was going up from the direction of the baseball diamond. The sounds pranced past like colored figures in a wild and lustrous pageant.

The reasons were never laid down formally, but Harold was pretty sure it was because of the triumph at the fair that he got his chance to become a member of Rouge the Red Taylor's gang. That, of course, and his great friendship with Dutch Reiseling. Of course his friendship with Dutch Reiseling was not wholly advantageous. Although the gang respected him for it, they also resented him a little. This was clear to them all.

They were all a little bigger than Harold was, all except Vince Hoffmeister, and Vince was notoriously tough for his size anyway. Vince could chew snoose and had once seen a colt being born and could walk over Russian thistles in his bare feet. Sometimes Harold was allowed to tag along behind the gang when they were collecting junk to sell to old Sam Goldblatt, or sweeping out empty grain cars for chicken feed to sell to the Chink. But when these public projects gave way to the club's secret activities, Harold's exclusion was automatic. They'd drift on up the railway tracks past the water tank, and turn off toward Webster's Ravine and Harold would know they were going to the secret hut and he'd stop and watch them go. They'd only had to tell him once, and there hadn't been any trouble then. "This gang is the Fierceless Five, see? That means only five can belong. See?" Harold saw.

This day Rouge and Doc Bailey had a fight. Not a fist fight, but a wrestling fight, and they weren't even mad at first. But Doc got Rouge down the first time and pinned his shoulders, and that made Rouge sore, and although Rouge got Doc down two out of three, he was still sore when it was all over and the upshot of it was that Doc went home, with Rouge and the other kids yelling after him that he'd better stay home if he wanted to be a doggone sorehead.

When they started for Webster's Ravine Harold stayed close behind them. He thought he hadn't better go too far without getting it cleared officially, and when they reached the top of the ravine he said in a careless tone that came off pretty well: "Hey guys, you need another guy?"

Rouge the Red Taylor stopped and turned around, looking at Harold as though he'd had no suspicion he was there.

"Huh?"

"I just thought you might need another guy," Harold stammered.

"I donno," Rouge said vaguely, making it clear that the question hadn't been important enough to warrant any previous thought. "What do you other guys think? Do we need another guy?"

"Naw." Vince Hoffmeister's grunt was so unequivocal that Harold started to turn back toward the town.

"Just a minute," Rouge said.

Harold came back quickly. Although he was not a member, Harold was familiar enough with the protocol that governed the gang's deliberations to know that this remark required no comment from him. He stood still, every part of him as still as the moment itself.

Charlie Johnson said, "I say we take him."

"Maybe we should." Rouge was still talking in a thinking-out-loud tone, "but he's gotta prove himself first."

"I know," Vince Hoffmeister suggested, "let's make him take a swim in the water tank." The water tank was a place of unique horror. One time—the section foreman kept his tools inside and nearly always left the door unlocked—six or seven of them had sneaked inside the massive red tube and climbed ninety-eight counted rungs up its vertical ladder to stand on a circular catwalk, staring down into a pool of ebony water, their whispers vaulting hollowly off its dead filmed surface. But nobody had dared to go into the water. Harold had reached over the side and broken the surface with one finger and drawn back suddenly, as sure as there can be sureness in any uncharted terror that the water had clutched at him and sought to drag him down.

"All right." The words were none of his doing. They forced themselves through his dry numbed lips, and he knew at once that they had lied.

"Aw, that's ree-dic," Charlie Johnson said uneasily. "That's absobloodyposolutely nuts."

"I know!" Rouge Taylor cried. "I know!"

"What, Rouge?" Harold yelled recklessly. "What you guys want me to do?"

"You'll do what we say if we let you in?"

"Sure, Rouge."

"Honest?"

"Honest!" He was pretty sure they weren't going to make him go in the water tank. He was pretty sure he could do anything else.

"You won't try to chicken out?"

"Honest I won't, Rouge."

"All right. This is what you do. Go up to Shea's and swipe five nut bars and bring 'em back here."

At first he had difficulty in assessing the new suggestion. It was less terrible than the other one, but more foreign; it lay in a new area, not yet even tentatively surveyed. He glanced briefly toward Charlie Johnson. Charlie wasn't precisely on his side, but if Charlie thought the new suggestion was suitable for consideration, perhaps it would be all right. Charlie said nothing.

"You going to do it?" Rouge challenged.

"Sure. I just never did it before. I got to figure it out first —don't I, guys?"

"Figure-it-out-figure-it-out," Vince Hoffmeister mocked. "If you swipe five nut bars you swipe five nut bars. What's there to figure out about that?"

"Aw bugger." Harold said this very softly and reflectively, not addressing it to anyone in particular, nor seeking to attach any relevance to it. He used it as a straight bid for time, an interim badge of manliness which might give him a few extra moments to straighten out his thoughts.

"Aw, you're scared of getting caught," Vince Hoffmeister jeered.

"I'm not."

"Old man Shea's so dopy he couldn't catch a cold," Vince Hoffmeister bragged. "I done it lotsa times. Didn't I, Rouge?"

"Tell him how," Rouge ordered.

"It's easy." Vince was now so heavy with self-importance that he'd become almost friendly. "He keeps them right up on the counter. He's always out in the back and it always takes him a while to come after he hears the bell. All you do is walk past once to make sure there's nobody inside."

Harold ran his tongue along his lower lip. "After he comes doesn't it look funny if you don't buy anything?"

"All you do," Vince was being very patient, "is ask him for licorice whips. He don't keep licorice whips."

Harold didn't want to seem to be arguing. It was not with the intention of arguing that he asked his next question; it was only to seek reassurance. He was desperately afraid they'd laugh, but he still had to ask.

"What about the Bible?" He controlled his voice very carefully, making the question a philosophical one, of no great practical significance but interesting enough to discuss. "You know—where it says 'Thou shalt not steal'?"

"Aw, that!"

Rouge Taylor's words, half scornful and half uneasy, were like the muffled closing of a door. If it had ever been a joke, it couldn't be a joke any longer.

"One time I heard it's only swiping if it's no more than two bits." Harold looked anxiously at their faces for confirmation. He knew now that this was all he had a right to expect. Charlie Johnson was the only one who met his eyes, and Charlie looked away in a hurry.

"I heard that too," Charlie mumbled, afraid to commit himself further, but willing to offer what comfort he could.

"Well, I guess I'll get started," Harold announced. There was no acknowledgment of this. The other four boys had turned away and, without speaking, had begun picking up pebbles from the gravel railway bed and throwing them up against the water tank, seeing who could throw the highest. Whatever Harold chose to do from now on was his own business. It had no connection with them.

"I guess I'll get started," he announced once more. He started up the track, neither hurrying nor taking too much time, just walking normally and counting the railway ties beneath his feet. When he reached the intersection between the track and the main street and turned up the street, he counted the boards on the sidewalk. He counted to himself, with deep concentration, making the numbers stomp loudly through his mind. At first the numbers excluded everything else. But as he drew nearer to the corner, menacing little chinks began to appear in his wall of concentration, and the piled-up thoughts at the other side of it darted savagely into the chinks. *Twenty-two. Twenty-two. Twenty-three. Twenty-three. Thou Shalt. Twenty-four. Twenty-four. Not steal. Twenty-five. Twenty-five. Twenty-six. Twenty-six. Thou shalt not join the gang. Twenty-seven. Twenty-seven. Twenty-eight. Twenty-eight. Only swiping. Only swiping. Twenty-nine. Twenty-nine.*

Shuffling along with his eyes glued on the sidewalk, he bumped into a man who stepped out of Morganson's store with a parcel under his arm. The man reached for Harold's shoulder to steady them both, and grunted a resentful "Hey!" Harold jumped away from him and ran across the street, time and the man's accusing look merged for him into some awful new dimension that, until he could stop and think it out, seemed to put what was about to happen into the same category as what had already happened and make his guilt an already completed fact.

He turned into the lane behind the post office and found a little sanctuary against the corner of a blackened high board fence. He leaned weakly against the fence and vomited, not urgently but rather absently and mechanically. He moved down the fence a few feet and closed his eyes tightly, trying to focus them inward on the white flood of his brain. By screwing his eyes tighter he could throw splashes of color across the flood, first blacks and grays, and then vivid reds and greens, none absolutely pure but all flecked and streaked with piercing incandescent yellows. This was not a prayer exactly, or at any rate he did not dare formalize it as a prayer, but he was hoping it would turn into a prayer of its own accord, or perhaps even a vision. Still nothing came into his mind but the white flood and its racing overtones.

He opened his eyes and walked back up the lane. He turned the corner briskly. He was inside the store without being conscious of opening the door.

The store was empty. He lurched against the counter. His hands were trembling and clumsy. He grabbed two Sweet Marie chocolate bars from the box at the front of the counter and stuffed them inside the neck of his cotton jersey, their brittle, crinkly wrappings rustling like giant wings. He reached into a box of Eatmors. The flat bars lay in an even layer, with no room between for a fingerhold. He pawed at a little crack on their surface, and just as one bar came away he saw Mr. Shea standing there in front of him on the other side of the counter, not five feet away. He jerked his hand back and the box of bars fell to the floor, scattering around his feet. For a long instant he looked full in Mr. Shea's face, a thin, very gray bloodless face with watery blue eyes and a thin mouth hidden by a fine gray overhanging mustache. Then he looked at Mr. Shea's old black sweater coat which hung on Mr. Shea's thin shoulders in long folds and had two big holes in the front.

"They fell," Harold babbled. He added, as though in explanation, "They must of fell or something."

Mr. Shea looked at him. The old man's watery eyes were two shallow stagnant pools, as barren of expression as of depth. Then as they held Harold's eyes in a numb clinch, a frightening ghostly feeling superimposed itself on the main layer of Harold's fright. This was almost supernatural, beyond God or the law; suddenly Harold sensed that the look in Mr. Shea's eyes was the same as the look that must be staring back from his own, a look of emptiness and insufficiency, the look of the dispossessed and lonely.

The old man broke the silence. "What's your name?"

Harold did not answer.

"I know anyway," Mr. Shea snapped. "You're that new family."

"We been here nearly six months." There had been no real accusation in Mr. Shea's voice, yet the need to offer a defense against the charge of belonging to a new family seemed even more urgent than the still undisposed matter of the chocolate bars.

"Maybe you got an excuse after all." The old man's words were loud and tremulous, with a kind of seedy power. Mr. Shea had drawn himself up until his thin chest almost filled the sagging black sweater, and patches of soiled white shirt showed through the holes. He quavered on like a pygmy Jehovah, full of pygmy omnipotence and pygmy compassion. "Maybe you thought you needed it, boy. I guess you don't get many candies, do you, boy?"

Harold made no reply.

"It's all right, boy," Mr. Shea was saying with pygmy kindness. "You can keep what you took. I won't tell." Carried away by the stunted grandeur of his part in the colloquy, Mr. Shea began to ramble: "We're all tempted. Blessed are the poor. Blessed are the poor. Say it after me, boy. Blessed are the poor."

Harold had backed up against the far wall of the musty little shop. He stole an anxious glance toward the door.

"Come on, boy. Say it and then you can go. Blessed are the poor."

"Blessed . . ." Harold tried, but the whisper died on his lips.

"Come on, boy!" Mr. Shea encouraged him anxiously.

Harold found himself thinking of Kally. He wished Kally were here now. She'd do something. She'd never submit to this terrible shame, no matter what. She was the littlest and she was the girl, but she'd never pretend to be fooled by this mean old man and his mean benevolence. No matter what it meant, Kally would never pretend that the situation was anything but what it was, anything but a mean old man trying to raise his own position among the helpless and the inconsequential by lowering someone else's position there.

"Come on, boy," Mr. Shea wheedled again. "Say it, boy. Blessed are the poor."

"I won't!" Harold quavered miserably. He lurched blindly through the door and ran home, his eyes stinging with tears of hate and desolation.

He was unable to go to school the next day. Guilt is not an easy affliction to get used to, especially for the innocent. He told his mother that he did not feel like eating and he told her that he felt a little weak and dizzy. In all this he told the literal truth and behind all this, crying piteously for release, was the larger, more dismal truth. But it was not the sort of truth that could be brought forth naked and unheralded, merely for the sake of shifting a burden of misery.

All morning he writhed and wallowed with the fear, which was only sometimes a fear and sometimes a hope, that Kally would come home at lunch time with some hint of his disgrace and that he would be thus forced to state at least its bare dimensions. He plied her nervously with leading questions and the only conclusion he was able to reach was that even Rouge the Red Taylor and his gang were unaware of the catastrophe which had befallen him, or, if aware of it, so stricken by its gravity that they had pledged themselves to secrecy.

There were so many permutations and combinations to consider that he could get no continuity into his thinking. He persuaded himself that nothing had happened because old Mr. Shea was giving him a second chance. Mr. Shea was probably waiting in his store right now, waiting for him to return and say the simple words he had been bidden to say and with that to bring the matter to an end. He persuaded himself that nothing had happened because Mr. Shea had summoned the district mounted policeman from Carsvale and nothing could happen before his arrival. He persuaded himself that Mr. Shea had only been trying to frighten him into a career of virtue and that, having seen how frightened he truly was, Mr. Shea, a good and generous man, was now content.

The day after that, a quiet September Saturday, Harold slept in exhausted until after nine o'clock. His mother shook him gently, sat on the side of his cot until she was certain he was entirely awake and then said in a mildly puzzled but unruffled voice: "Mr. Hollishaw is out in the kitchen, Harold. He says Mr. Grier would like to see you down at the library."

He knew at once—knew at once in a blending of utter relief and utter terror—that this announcement concerned the affair between him and Mr. Shea. But it was a moment before the symbols contained in the announcement could be fitted into place. Mr. Hollishaw, who rang the town bell at noon and at one o'clock and six o'clock, and who looked after the electric-light plant and the sidewalks, was the town constable, a representative of the law. Mr. Grier, who owned the barbershop, was also the local justice of the peace. The one-room public library was also the town hall and the courthouse.

Harold began to cry. His mother's firm arms drew him upright on the bed and she whispered. "Don't worry, Harold. I'm sure you haven't done anything very bad."

"But I have," he sobbed.

"Poof!" his mother reassured him. "Mr. Hollishaw told me a little about it. You're right to be sorry for it and I'm glad you're sorry, Harold. Now we'll just go down and see Mr. Grier and tell him exactly what happened, and everybody will feel a whole lot better."

His mother helped him dress and led him to the kitchen. Mr. Hollishaw, a small, wiry man of advanced years, was sitting on a kitchen chair staring uncomfortably at the floor while Kally, seated on another chair across the room, regarded him with grim-lipped contempt and accusation.

"Good morning, Harold," Mr. Hollishaw said defensively. "You ready to come now?"

"Can I come too, Mother?" Kally said, as though Mr. Hollishaw were not even in the room.

"Why, of course, dear," Mrs. Sondern said.

"Would you like me to get your cap, Harold?" Kally asked, looking at him warmly through Mr. Hollishaw.

"No, thanks," Harold answered politely.

Mr. Chatsworth was working in the garden. It was his day between runs. They went past him silently, Mr. Hollishaw walking quickly on ahead and tactfully refraining from looking back to see if they were following. Kally dropped behind for a moment and whispered with awful solemnity: "Harold's under arrest!"

Mr. Chatsworth dropped his Dutch hoe. "What!"

"We're going to the trial," Kally said importantly. She searched his florid, bewildered face for any stray portents of disaster. "They better not try anything funny, that's all," she said less certainly, and ran off to catch up with the other two.

There were not more than thirty people in the low-ceilinged rectangular room when they entered. Harold did not dare look at any of them, much less attempt to count them, but after Mr. Hollishaw had seated them along a special row of chairs beside the massive oaken table that filled the end of the room furthest from the door, both Kally and Mrs. Sondern looked around them with respectful interest. "Quite a few in from north of town," Mrs. Sondern whispered. "I guess the rain the other night's still holding up the threshing. They didn't get a drop south of the valley." Occasionally she exchanged a politely formal nod with someone in the back of the room. "There's poor old Mrs. Banks. Remind me to ask her about her towels, Kally. They seem to have got mixed up with Mrs. Russell's, the poor old soul." The faces of the spectators were friendly and not unduly prying. On the other hand they were not embarrassed or self-consciously withdrawn. It was plain that no one expected anything particularly exciting to happen; still, something was going to happen and the right to witness it was universal and unchallengeable.

At last Mr. Grier bustled in, a slight bald-headed man with a thin, brown mustache. Mr. Shea pattered along at his side, equally slight and bald-headed. Mr. Grier waved him to a seat near the table, directly opposite where Harold sat. He himself sat down in the wooden armchair behind the table. He took off his rimless glasses, put them on the table in front of him, cast a dignified beam on the audience, and then turned to Harold and said: "Is your name Harold Sondern?"

It came so abruptly that Harold, who had been counting the cracks in the floor to fill the hideous void in his mind, could not at first believe he had heard correctly. "Is your name Harold Sondern?"

"That's right, Mr. Grier," Harold heard his mother announce pleasantly.

Mr. Grier glanced anxiously toward the spectators. Apparently satisfied that his position had not been diminished in their eyes, he permitted himself a generous smile and said gently: "Try and answer for yourself, son."

"Yes, sir," Harold said.

"These proceedings are not formal," Mr. Grier announced. "No legal complaint has been made and no witnesses will be legally sworn. This court has always sought to abide by the principle that what is good is just and that the accomplishment of good should not be restricted by the mere forms of justice."

Harold looked up with interest. A benign and salty timbre had entered Mr. Grier's voice. He sounded exactly like Lionel Barrymore.

"Now, Harold," Mr. Grier continued, "the court wishes you to understand that no harm shall befall you here. It appears that on the late afternoon of September 9 you attempted to commit a violation of the law at the expense of one of your—ah—fellow citizens. This fellow citizen has not chosen to invoke the law against you and the court applauds him for his humanity. It is his belief, and the court agrees, however, that it would be well for you, Harold, and for the community in which you dwell if you could be brought to a clear understanding of your error and to some knowledge of the trouble which that sort of error can bring to you if it is repeated."

A stentorian clap of sound intruded on the silence of the spectators' benches. Mr. Grier paused, glaring. Harold looked around timidly. Mr. Chatsworth, of whose presence in the room he had not been aware, was seated in the back row; now he was carefully folding a navy blue handkerchief and placing it in the inside pocket of his navy blue suit coat.

"Now, Harold," Mr. Grier said, "do you admit that on the evening of September 9 you entered the business premises of Mr. Kevin Shea and attempted to steal a quantity of confectionery?"

Harold had returned to his study of the floor. He understood the nature of the question, but he no longer understood the nature of the answer which he was expected to give. The kindly, cleansing words which had preceded the question had apparently been intended to make some sort of technical distinction, to show him that although he had been nominally in the wrong, the names for what he had done and for what ought to be done with him on its account must be chosen very carefully. Mr. Grier had gone to such pains to explain the hidden meanings that he did not want to upset them with a sudden, blurted word. As he grappled with the problem of what to say, it occurred to him that perhaps Mr. Grier had been trying to tell him the very same thing he had been trying to tell himself during the long and lonely walk from the water tank to the store of Mr. Shea. If it's not more than a quarter it isn't stealing; it's only swiping.

Mr. Grier leaned forward. "Do you admit, Harold, that you tried to steal a quantity of confectionery from the store of Mr. Shea?"

"No, sir," Harold said.

Mr. Grier had already begun to form his next remark before he fully realized what Harold had said. His open mouth quivered soundlessly.

"What?" Mr. Grier said.

"No, sir," Harold said. "I didn't."

Someone at the back of the room giggled.

"Order!" Mr. Grier demanded uncertainly. He leaned across the table sternly. "This is a very serious matter, young man," he said. "A very, very serious matter indeed. The court will not countenance lying, young man. Do you hear that, Harold? The court will not countenance lying."

It was worse than his blackest dreams. Harold shut his eyes tightly and grasped the edges of his chair. He tried to shut everything away from his mind, Mr. Grier and his mother and Kally and Mr. Shea and the people in the back of the room. He clung to the chair, denying existence to everything except the chair's cold, hard edges.

"Now," Mr. Grier said. "Please reconsider your answer."

Harold felt his mother's hand on his arm. He kept his eyes closed and his body stiffened, merging into the lifeless sanctuary of the chair.

"Answer me!" Mr. Grier commanded hoarsely. "Answer me, Harold."

"Don't answer him!" a louder, hoarser voice commanded, almost directly on top of Mr. Grier's voice. "Don't say anything."

The room's center of gravity swirled away from Mr. Grier toward the direction of the new voice. It was an irresistible process, so irresistible that even Harold opened his eyes and turned them, with the other eyes, to the back of the room. There William Chatsworth had rumbled to his feet and now towered high against the square frame of the room's single window, like a purple giant in stained glass.

"Order!" Mr. Grier shouted. "The court must . . ."

"What court?" Mr. Chatsworth rumbled angrily. "You said yourself this has nothing to do with the law."

"Remove him," Mr. Grier commanded the constable, Mr. Hollishaw.

Mr. Hollishaw scraped to his feet and pattered across the room and stood in front of Mr. Chatsworth, as bold and ready to spring away as a terrier challenging a strange mastiff. "You'll have to go," he intimated. Mr. Chatsworth ignored him.

"You said you didn't want to hurt this boy," Mr. Chats-

worth said angrily. "And yet you bring him here, in front
of everybody, and you hurt him in front of everybody for
the sake of proving that you aren't going to hurt him. Why
didn't you just have a talk with him if you didn't want to
hurt him?"

"The court . . ."

"There isn't any court."

"Perhaps," Mr. Grier said bitterly, "you would prefer that
these proceedings were discontinued and resumed at a later
date under the full processes of the law?"

"If you mean by that," Mr. Chatsworth said, "that you're
going to drag this boy into a legal court with a legal warrant,
I think you'd better think it over. I'll see that he has a good
lawyer. And if things go badly for him, I'll see that the case
is appealed. I'll see that it's appealed right up and down the
province and right up and down the country as long as I've
got one red cent. All the way to the Privy Council, if it takes
my last cent. And it won't be this boy that's on trial, Billy
Grier. It will be you that's on trial, you and your stupidity
and your phony mercy."

Mr. Chatsworth had taken his big gold railroad watch
from his vest pocket and was bouncing it furiously in the
palm of his big red hand. "I'm sorry if I hurt your feelings,"
he called to the front of the room. "I know it's hard for you
to resist the temptation to make a big man of yourself in
public. But you shouldn't try to make a big man of yourself
at the expense of little boys."

"How can you say that?" Mr. Grier cried in an agony of
virtue. He repeated the question beseechingly to the room
at large: "How can he say that?"

No one answered him. The people in the back of the room
were already rising from their chairs and drifting quickly toward the street, their faces averted, simulating incompre-
hension, like people who have blundered into the wrong
bathroom. Everybody was leaving him, even the constable,

Mr. Hollishaw, who had pattered to the door under the pretext of directing traffic. Mr. Grier looked longingly at Mrs. Sondern. Mrs. Sondern smiled at him sympathetically and said: "Is it all right for us to go too, Mr. Grier?"

"I suppose so," Mr. Grier groaned. He grasped at a tiny remnant of dignity and said severely: "I hope the boy has learned his lesson."

"I'm sure he has," Mrs. Sondern assured him gently. "I'm sure he has."

They walked home together through the village, none of them trying to comment on what had occurred. It was much too strange and complicated for talk.

Chapter Twelve

Mr. Chatsworth did not go directly home. He walked alone across the September hills to the cool brown river that ran below the town and sat beside it for more than an hour chunking pebbles into the water.

Thus Amelia Chatsworth did not hear of his bizarre and alien act from her husband's own lips. This in itself was a humiliation, but it was as nothing compared to the humiliation of the act itself.

"If you only could have seen Billy Grier's *face!*" her neighbor and good friend, Bertha Jessup, recounted, peering treacherously into Amelia's face for each tiny flicker of torment and masked fury.

"Yes," Amelia said.

"Such a warmhearted man," Bertha Jessup taunted generously. "My Bob's the very soul of consideration, I couldn't ask for a better husband, but I honestly believe he'd no more think of jumping off Niagara Falls than do a thing like that."

"Yes," Amelia Chatsworth said. Neither would Bill, her tortured spirit cried within. Neither would Bill. And yet, even as she writhed in protest, she reminded herself that this had been ordained long ago, that she had seen it coming and had not raised a hand to prevent it. Vanessa rushing from her, hastening with every sign of gladness to that sweating baseball man. And now Bill. All ordained and nothing done to stop it.

It had been ordained from the outset of that winter morning, when the hermetic, hygienic, feeling-proof sheathing that bound their lives together had been torn apart to let the strangers in. It had been more than twenty years in the making, it had become a thing of perfection, a model to be exclaimed upon wherever the models of matrimony were held in reverence. "Such a wonderful man"—no one had put it more suitably than the treacherous Bertha Jessup herself —"he never seems to go anywhere or do anything, does he? And Vanessa, such a wonderful daughter! Never happy unless she's home!" And now it lay in ruins, fit only for polite mockery and clucking sidelong memories.

There was no discussion of any kind between them. The only reference to the matter was singularly oblique. On Sunday afternoon Kally and Harold were playing noisily on the porch. Mr. Chatsworth stamped angrily to the door, flung it open and shouted: "Stop that racket right away!" But Amelia was not in the least disarmed; the affront to her intelligence merely aggravated the larger, irreparable affront.

Late in the afternoon, while her husband was dozing on the sofa, she saw Mrs. Sondern moving about the big back yard, mending a clothesline in preparation for Monday's washing. She stood at the kitchen window speculatively and then slipped outside and joined her.

"A lovely day, isn't it?" she said nervously.

"Just grand. I always think September's the finest month anyway, don't you?"

Mrs. Chatsworth drew in her breath like a swimmer preparing to submerge and said quickly: "Have you heard from your husband recently?"

Mrs. Sondern dropped her eyes to the knot she was making. "Not since that night last week." She looked up with a calm, even smile. "Poof! More like morning. That man never has the slightest idea of time. I'm sorry he woke you up. He never does have the slightest idea of . . ."

"Don't mention it. I was just thinking that there's all the room in the world right here. We could easily open up the front room upstairs."

"That's very kind of you," Mrs. Sondern said, her voice guarded and puzzled.

"Well then, why don't you drop him a note and suggest . . ."

"But we'd pretty well decided it would save time and extra moving and extra expense and all if he stayed in Dobie until he got our affairs wound up and then we all went on right away."

"It's certainly a chore, isn't it?" Mrs. Chatsworth sighed companionably.

"Well, there isn't really so very much left to do in Dobie. I think as far as getting the furniture packed and selling off the odds and ends he's got all that pretty well done. But this friend of his, this Mr. Brannick that he's been staying with, I think he's had a setback in his health or something and Chris doesn't feel like leaving him until he's back on his feet."

It was the first really confidential talk the two women had had. Mrs. Chatsworth was reveling in it, with the delight that comes of discovering bottomless perfidy in an enemy. She probed deeper into the gloriously vile abyss, reinforcing and sanctifying her bitterness.

"I suppose that may be some time yet," Mrs. Chatsworth said.

"Oh no, I don't think so. Chris is just as anxious to get up there as the rest of us. It was really his idea, you know.

If Mr. Brannick isn't better soon, I imagine Chris will arrange for somebody else to look after him."

Oh, the lies! The lies! The black and lovely lies! "Well," Mrs. Chatsworth said, with something close to genuine amiability, "I guess I'd better go and get the roast in."

She was scarcely able to sleep for excitement. In the morning she said good-by to her husband with impatient cordiality. As soon as she had seen him through the gate with his little black bag, she hurried to the telephone in the living room.

"Long distance," she said. "I want to talk to Mr. Sondern in Dobie. He's at the Brannick farm."

At first Chris was of two minds whether to answer or not. It would be for Brannick, of course, and Brannick was watering the horses while Chris boiled the coffee and fried the eggs. But the party signal was repeated a second time and then a third time, and he went listlessly to the corner and picked up the receiver.

"Yes, this is Sondern," he shouted eagerly when he heard the operator's voice asking for him and recognized the voice as the operator's in Elevator. "Hello, Bea!" he yelled. "Is that you Bea?" he yelled, trying to thrust aside the operator's voice with the strength and urgency of his own.

"This is Mrs. Chatsworth in Elevator. Can you hear me?"

"I can hear you," Chris shouted. "Talk a little louder. Where's Bea? Where's my wife?"

"She's not here just now. I just called to say . . ."

"Where is she?" Chris shouted. "Where has Bea gone?"

"She's getting the children ready for school."

"Well, I want to talk to Bea. What's the matter? What's happened?"

"Now listen carefully, Mr. Sondern. I . . ."

"I *am* listening!" Chris shouted. "Why can't I talk to Bea? Why are you calling me at nine o'clock in the morning?"

"Well, at least I'm not calling at one o'clock in the morning," the distant voice said resentfully.

"You never mind that. If I telephoned anybody at one o'clock in the morning I telephoned my wife."

"For heaven's sake, Mr. Sondern . . ."

"For heaven's sake is what *I* say," Chris shouted, his voice breaking with exasperation and suspense. Suddenly he realized he was not making sense. His head was seething and muddled. "Just a minute, please," he said, "I'll be right back."

He hurried across the room and reached above the kitchen table for the rye bottle. He pawed the top loose and took a long red soothing drink from the neck of the bottle.

"I'm sorry if I got a little excited," he said when he had returned to the telephone. "I just got up. I guess I was still half asleep."

"That's all right, Mr. Sondern. Now please listen very carefully. There's nothing for you to worry about. Perhaps I shouldn't be calling you, but I think there's something you ought to know."

"Yes?"

"Now there's nothing to worry about, not in this particular thing. It's just that, well, the boy, he's been in a little bit of trouble and . . ."

"What kind of trouble? What's happened to him?"

"Now, there's nothing to worry about, just a little thing about trying to take some candy from a store. But I thought you'd want to know; I'm only saying this because Mrs. Sondern and the children are living here with us and all, and . . ."

"Why didn't my wife telephone me? Why are you calling? Why didn't she call?"

"Well, I really can't say about that, Mr. Sondern. I just thought . . ."

"You think I ought to come up there to Elevator," Chris said. "Isn't that what you're getting at?"

"I don't know, Mr. Sondern. That's not my business. But if it was my son . . ."

"Does Bea know about this? Does she know you're talking to me? Did she have anything to do with you calling me?"

"Well, no. At least I don't suppose she did. Not directly."

"What are you trying to say to me then?" Chris shouted. "Why are you saying it?" He had lost control over his voice again. "Does Bea want me to come up there or not? Did she say so or not?"

"Well, perhaps not in so many words. It's just that I think they're going away tomorrow, going north I understood her to say, and . . ."

"Going!" Chris shouted.

"Not that I'm sure. Not absolutely."

"Did she say I should come?" Chris repeated almost angrily.

"Well——"

"How do you know then?" he shouted. "How then?"

"Just different things she's let drop now and then."

"What things?"

"Oh, just different things. I can't remember what exactly."

"Listen, Mrs.—what did you say your name was again?"

"Mrs. Chatsworth."

Chris had meant to say, Listen, Mrs. Chatsworth, I know you're lying. But for a moment he said nothing. With the realization that she was lying, his fever of excitement died. The little instant of exaltation sputtered out. For the moment nothing was important except the desert fact that he had been almost induced to believe his family wanted him and that he now knew the belief to have been false. His numbness of spirit was so overpowering that he had neither the heart to reproach her for the lie nor the curiosity to explore its reason.

"Well, thanks for calling me, Mrs. Chatsworth," he mumbled.

"Will you be coming?" she asked anxiously.

"I don't know," he said. "I'll have to think it over." He hung up slowly, without saying good-by.

When he left the telephone he had not intended to think it over at all. He had intended to put the whole thing away from him, to treat it as something that had never happened. When Roxy came in for breakfast he did not mention the matter at all. And when Roxy went out again to mend a fence on the south quarter section, Chris fended off the temptation to think of it by finding half a dozen jobs to do around the house and barn and attacking them with all his energy. But the heavy exertion tired and weakened him and before the morning was half over he found it necessary to pause for a rest. He sat in the armchair in the kitchen with a small drink in his hand and began going over the conversation, a fragment at a time, now re-examining a sentence, now recalling some particular timbre in the woman's voice, now withdrawing stonily from the whole subject, only to find himself coming back to it with querulous surprise.

It was now out of Mrs. Chatsworth's hands. There had been a moment during the conversation on the telephone when she had experienced a chill of actual physical fright. She was accustomed to thinking in symbols and to her the missing misguided husband of Beatrice Sondern had had no significance or identity except as a symbol. He was a part of a train of events that had come into her life, a vital part to be sure, for in order to control, redirect and expel those events from her life, it had become essential that she obtain some control over him. But she had pictured him only in the abstract, as something alien but faceless, a hostile circumstance. Because of the circumstance of his being, her aspirations and her pride had been placed in unbearable jeopardy; she had seen a way to remove the jeopardy by making use of the circumstance.

The man had unnerved her momentarily by refusing to play the role of a circumstance. The quick shivering cascades of hope and disbelief, of doubt and anxiety, of excitement and dismay, had invested his far-off voice with something eerie and unreckoned. It was like hearing a piece of furniture cry out in pain.

She had to sit down for a while, recapitulating the justness of her position before she was prepared to call on Mrs. Sondern. She thought it best to come to the point.

"I was talking to your husband."

"Oh yes," Mrs. Sondern said. Her eyes fluttered about the upstairs kitchen like two dark bewildered birds frightened suddenly from cover and seeking a place to hide. They lighted on an empty chair. "Won't you sit down?"

"I think he's on his way here," Mrs. Chatsworth said stolidly.

"Oh," Mrs. Sondern gasped weakly and sat down on the proffered chair herself. "You made him," she said dully. "He wouldn't come unless somebody made him. He knows it's bad for everybody. You made him."

"I thought you'd want to know," Mrs. Chatsworth's voice seemed to be leaning slightly forward in an attitude of anxious peering.

"Yes," Mrs. Sondern said.

"He seemed to think it was his place to be here. He seemed to think that with the trouble over Harold . . ."

"Shh," Mrs. Sondern said. "I have to think."

"You haven't any call to talk to me like that."

"There isn't any call to talk at all," Mrs. Sondern said in a soft, pleading whisper. She got up slowly from her chair, walked downstairs to the telephone and asked for the station. "Could you please tell me the fare to Moose Jaw?" she asked.

"Thank you very much." She walked upstairs again and hauled the frayed wicker suitcase from beneath the kitchen couch, opened it on the table, and began moving about the two rooms filling it with clothing. Mrs. Chatsworth remained standing hesitantly near the doorway.

"I haven't started the laundry," Mrs. Sondern said. "It's all marked, except Mrs. Banks's. It's in the flowered bag. If you wouldn't mind seeing that it goes back . . ."

"Are you going?" Mrs. Chatsworth asked, feeling she must say something.

"I wish I could have said good-by to Mr. Chatsworth." Mrs. Sondern sighed. "I wish I could have thanked him. I don't suppose you'd like to thank . . ." She stopped and looked doubtfully at the older woman. And then she moved to her side and touched her compassionately on the arm. Mrs. Chatsworth allowed her hand to rest there for a moment and then turned and glided swiftly through the doorway.

Automatically, as though in response to a reflex, Mrs. Sondern went to the bureau drawer and brought her worn black purse to the table. She emptied and confirmed its contents, two ten-dollar bills, a five, a two, and six ones and forty cents in change, and made a calculation on the back of an envelope. The result seemed to please her, for she did not dwell upon it. Instead she sat for a few moments, making a pretended rendezvous with her husband, enriching the rich days of their first quiet years while she made ready to depart from him again.

She worked briskly through the brief remainder of the morning. She took down all the dishes from the shelves, washed them carefully and put them back in place, and then scrubbed the two floors. She was just drying her hands when the children exploded in on her from the top of the stairway.

"Last-one-home's-a-stinker-Harold-is-a-stinker!" Kally was singing jubilantly. She braked herself on the still damp linoleum. "Hey, isn't this washday? Hey, where's the washing?"

"Cheat! She tripped me!" Harold's yell was a few feet behind. "Hey!"

"Hey, Hey! How many heys to make a haystack?" Mrs. Sondern presented her most mysterious smile.

"The suitcase!" Kally shouted. "Look, Harold! The suitcase! We're going somewhere."

"Aw no." Harold's ardent face sagged into a picture of disbelief and protest. "Aw no, Mother. We can't go away now."

"Just because he's on Rouge the Red Taylor's ball team." Kally's tone both belittled and boasted. "They chose up sides at recess and Harold was the third one picked."

"What are we going away for, Mother?" Harold exhorted desperately.

"My goodness, listen to that, would you. Listen to old off-again-on-again-Finnegan."

"Begin again," Kally giggled.

"Aw now, come on," Harold protested. "All I wanted was to go all the way. But we still can't go all the way. Why don't we just stay here until we can go all the way at once?"

"I vote for Harold," Kally said, suddenly surrendering to logic.

"You're going to think I'm the silliest thing that ever lived." Mrs. Sondern shook her head lugubriously. "But I clean forgot about excursion rates."

"What excursion rates?" Harold demanded suspiciously.

"Why the excursion rates to Moose Jaw. This is the very last day for the fall excursions and if we don't go right today it will cost us twice as much."

"But what do we have to go to Moose Jaw for anyway?"

"My goodness, Harold, it's on the way. It's all that much closer, isn't it?"

"Anyway," Harold objected, "excursion tickets aren't any good unless you buy them return."

"And there's so much more opportunity in Moose Jaw," his mother went on quickly. "There'll be all sorts of things to do."

"I vote for Mother," Kally said. "I vote for Moose Jaw."

"By spring we won't have to worry about their silly old excursion rates," Mrs. Sondern pointed out. "Not after we once get to Moose Jaw. We'll sail right on through by Pullman. Pullman, poof! I wouldn't be surprised if we went the rest of the way by airplane."

Harold was staring stonily at the floor, fiercely resisting the risk of infection. "Let's stay here," he begged abjectly. "Let's just stay here till Christmas anyway."

Mrs. Sondern looked sorrowfully from his miserable face to the clock above the kitchen stove. Kally had slipped into the bedroom to rummage for a long-neglected doll.

"Harold," Mrs. Sondern whispered, "you know we wouldn't be going unless there was a very good reason." Her eyes rested on his, beseeching him not to make her say more.

They hurried down the noontime-emptied street and caught the train to Moose Jaw with five minutes to spare.

Kally first insisted on kissing Mrs. Chatsworth good-by, and Mrs. Chatsworth insisted on giving her a new dollar bill for herself and another one for Harold.

Chapter Thirteen

Chris clanked heroically out of Roxy Brannick's place in that same late afternoon. It had taken him some hours to make his decision. Then he had rolled a clean shirt, a fresh pair of socks and a new bottle of whisky into the back section of the Leader-Post, trotted unsteadily across the yard to the 1934 Chevrolet, and begun his journey. A moment earlier he had been telling himself over and over again that he wasn't going to go at all, that there were no reasons why he should go and many reasons why he shouldn't, but once the decision to go was achieved, speed became the core of the whole enterprise. He slammed into gear and stamped on the accelerator the instant the engine caught, and the back wheels churned into the dusty yard as though on a tread-mill before they took hold and sprang toward the gate. He almost lost his grip of the steering wheel during this first headlong lunge, and the right-hand door, which he had neglected to close, clanged against a fence post like a hollow anvil. Roxy ran out of the barn, shouting and waving his arms, but Chris kept his foot on the floor.

Now that he had made his decision, he saw the inevitability of it. There was even a certain spiritual luxury, as when a man decides to die for some higher good. Chris was certain in this moment that all of heaven and all its indistinct angels intended him now to repossess the white lovely body of his wife and true love, Beatrice Sondern, and to be caressed and claimed by her in turn.

There were matters here involved that no one but he and Bea could understand or even dream about. One time in Regina, when there were only the two of them, when there were no children, there had been a gray flannel sheet on their big and slightly lumpy double bed. Many and many a time as they lay quiet and together after they had earned their quiet on this gray flannel sheet, Chris would let his arm fall across the smooth cool body of his wife and meet the comforting warmth of the flannel sheet beyond. In these moments he felt as close to ultimate meaning as a man could hope to be. It was difficult to believe that he would ever be happy again. It was equally difficult to believe that he would ever be unhappy again. And the years brought no change; whatever had done violence to his life and his dream, Chris had never found a name for it. Bea was lovelier and more splendid after Harold. She was still lovelier and more splendid after Kally. The loss was of his imagining and his foolish despair. There was no loss, no loss at all, except in his own mind. He made the car go faster.

It had grown dark. A jack rabbit ran in and out of his headlights and reminded him that the road had ditches. He slowed down and hunched over the wheel and peered on into the empty beckoning night. The woman in Elevator had spoken of the boy. She had spoken of Harold. She had no right to do that. She had been unfair. It was bitter enough to hear the distant stifled cry of Bea falling away forever in the ebb of drying years. To hear Harold and Kally too was much more than was fair. He stole a glance at the gas gauge. It wavered at just above a quarter full. He drew a fresh bead on the gravel road ahead and stamped the pedal down as far as it would go.

The night grew quite black. There was nothing to guide him now, nothing but a star off to the right that danced from white to orange and that he had often looked at as a boy and told his fellow boys was the evening star. He decided to follow only one thing, the two clumsy fingers of the gravel road leaping up beneath his headlights.

He crouched lower over the wheel. Suddenly he found himself, without dramatics or apparent incident of any kind, in the middle of a stubble field with the remnants of a two-strand barbed-wire fence clinging to the rear fender. He knew that he was almost sober because it was not even necessary to walk back to the road for him to ascertain that he had missed the jog of a correction line.

He got back into the car and raced the motor, but the wheels merely dug themselves into the soft stubble field. Now he became frightened. They may be gone, he told himself. I must get there now. If I don't get there by morning, I'll never see them again. Bea! Bea! I love you. I'll die.

He put the car in reverse gear and got out and tried pushing it. The sweat broke slowly and then began to blind him. He kept rocking the car, and once he thought he almost had it moving, but it only sank deeper into the mud.

He stumbled over to the car and sank down on the edge of the running board and put his head between his hands. He sat there hopelessly. He sat there on the edge on an old automobile that he had stolen and thought of a woman that he had lost and of a boy that he had lost and a girl that he had lost.

And then suddenly, far in the distance, he saw a light. It was a light that he could aspire to and a light that he might even reach. It was the light of a farmhouse, not more than a mile away. He began to walk toward the light. As he walked, he began to cry. Not dramatically or self-consciously, but quietly. If his tears had any immediate origin, their origin was gratitude. For he knew that by great good luck he would be able to get Roxy Brannick's car out of the ditch and with the help of the three gallons of gas still left to him he would be able to get to Elevator, Saskatchewan, and speak to his wife Beatrice and his son Harold and his daughter Kathleen, and arrange a better life among them than they could ever have if they went away again without him and left him here in this forgotten ditch.

It was more difficult walking toward the distant light than he had thought it would be. Once he fell through the steepness of a rut. Once he had to climb a fence which proved to be of barbed wire and he had to tear himself away from it with a gash in his leg. Then for the last half mile he trudged across a dark and barren field. Once he fell on his knees, having stumbled on a rock. Once a huge dog came and snarled at him and would only go away when Chris—though greatly terrified—stooped down and grabbed a stone and snarled back.

At last he reached the farmhouse. The distant light had changed from orange to white. Enfeebled by mud and exertion and drink, Chris tapped on the door. A very huge and very malevolent man, a man with no hair and huge eyebrows, was suddenly glaring at him behind a halo of electric power. He leaned close to Chris, inspecting him with his eyes and his nose.

"I'm sorry," Chris panted, "but I ran off the road at the concession line."

The man with the eyebrows peered at Chris and sniffed at him. He sniffed again.

"Bugger off!"

Then he closed the door. Chris was alone in the night. Behind him was the ruined automobile. Ahead were Bea and Harold and Kally, about to rush from all the parts of the world that he had ever heard of and would ever know. He walked a little unsteadily toward the gate again. But before he reached the gate some great and courageous feeling took hold of him and he turned around and walked back and knocked on the door of the farmhouse again.

The man with the eyebrows answered once more and said once more, only louder this time: "I said bugger off!" He made as though to close the door. Chris put his thin hand inside, but the man thrust Chris's hand outside again and jammed the door shut. Chris turned, this time completely defeated, and trudged once more to the gate. But again, as he turned his eye to the great white star above his head, he felt the need to return to the farmhouse once more. He fell down once, but picked himself up with great dignity. He pounded on the door. The man with the eyebrows hovered above him in majestic wrath. "Go away!" the man with the eyebrows thundered. "Go away, or I'll eat your bloody guts!"

Chris had no feeling of cowardice or heroism or of volition of any kind. All he knew now was that his car was stuck in a ditch and that the man with the eyebrows had to get his car out of the ditch.

"Come out and fight," Chris commanded. "Come out and fight."

The man with the eyebrows came out of the doorway with the light behind him, like a murderous gorilla emerging from a sunrise.

He put out a great hand and knocked Chris down. Chris got up and the man with the eyebrows knocked him down again. Chris got up once more. "All I want you to do," he said politely, spitting out a mouthful of blood and holding up his fists, "is to pull my car out of the ditch."

The man with the eyebrows knocked him down again.

Chris shouted: "I'll tear you apart, you dirty son of a bitch!" He now recognized that it was necessary to work himself into some form of rage. "I'll tear you apart!" he bragged.

The man with the eyebrows knocked him down again. Chris rose from the mud in a crouch and charged the man with the eyebrows head on, striking him in his generous belly with his head. The man with the eyebrows fell down and began cursing. Chris perceived that his adversary was tired and out of breath, even more so than he himself. So he straightened up and began kicking him in the stomach. The man with the eyebrows lurched to his feet, staggered back into the kitchen and clutched at the kitchen table. Chris picked up a chair and hit him over the arms with the chair, knocking him down again.

"Jesus Christ!" the man with the eyebrows whimpered. "Jesus Christ!"

"All I want you to do," Chris panted, "is get my car out of the ditch."

"Well, why didn't you say so?" the other man gasped, dragging himself grayly erect with the help of the kitchen sink. Then he floundered out to the barn and harnessed up a team of gray percherons and took them across the fields to where Roxy Brannick's car was stuck. The horses easily hauled the car back to the road. Chris gave the man two dollars.

When he got to Elevator it was past breakfast time and the last of the rye was gone. The first three or four people he asked to direct him to the Chatsworth house kept responding to his impatient questions with other, maddening questions of their own. One man wanted to know what he was doing driving a car with a flat tire, and another kept looking around the street, as though for help, and asking his name and where he came from. A fat, cross-eyed woman asked him point blank how much he had had to drink. In a flash of inspiration Chris stopped in front of the Chinese café and honked until the Chinaman came out. Chinamen had no sense of Christian outrage or municipal virtue. Chinamen were willing to live and let live. He asked the Chinaman how to get to the Chatsworth house and the Chinaman said without unnecessary comment that it was the first on the right at the top of the street.

He rushed up the steps to the porch and thumped at the door with both hands. The door was opened almost at once. Chris took only sufficient notice of the woman who stood in the gloomy inner vestibule to establish that she was not his wife. "Bea!" he called past her into the dark hallway. "Bea!" He started to move on past the woman.

"You can't come in here."

"Bea!" he called, walking straight ahead into the dark living room.

"You can't come in here like that. I won't have anyone in that condition . . ."

"Turn on the lights!" Chris shouted. "Somebody turn on the lights."

The woman's hand felt past him for the wall switch and her face, harsh with fright, swam into his ken like a yellow mask floating under water.

"Who're you? What're you doing here?" Chris demanded resentfully. His voice, long trained to speak through drink, was much clearer and steadier than his mind.

"I'm Mrs. Chatsworth. And if I were you, I'd just . . ."

"Where's Bea then? Where are my kids?"

"They're not here."

Chris saw the dark rectangle of the doorway to the kitchen and darted through it. "Turn on the light in here!" he shouted. Mrs. Chatsworth, protesting with timorous outrage, darted after him and complied. Chris ran down the hallway and into the ground-floor bedroom. The process was repeated there and then he stumbled up the stairway and the process was repeated again in each of the upstairs rooms.

He went down the stairs slowly, Mrs. Chatsworth following him in timid, angry silence. He sat down heavily on the sofa in the living room.

"They're gone," he said.

"Why don't you just go down to the hotel and get a good sleep?"

"She asked me to come," Chris said. "She *asked* me. Why isn't she here? She got some woman to phone up and ask me to come. Why isn't she here?"

"If you could just get a good . . ."

"Where'd they go?"

"I don't know."

"WHERE'D THEY GO?" Chris shouted it at the top of his lungs, not angrily or threateningly, but with the shrill misery of a lament rising from a dungeon.

Mrs. Chatsworth shrank against the wall and stared into his haggard, haunted face for a full second. "They were going to Grande Prairie, Alberta," she whimpered.

"No!" Chris said. "No!" The words were not much louder than a whisper, but they leaped with wonder and exaltation. "They really *are* going there! The Peace River Country! What do you know about that?"

He stared out the window into the sunny morning. "The Peace River Country," he said softly.

He sat on for a few moments, looking through the window, not saying anything. Then he rose from the sofa and walked toward the front door. He walked quickly at first, but his steps slowed uncertainly. When he reached the porch he came to a stop, hesitated there, and then turned back and ran into the house.

"What do you mean by saying that?" he rasped, white with fury. "It's too far! You thought you had me fooled, but I know how far it is."

"I think they were just going to Moose Jaw at first," she whimpered. "I think they were going to go on later."

"Sure," he said. "I should have figured that out." His heart had risen as quickly as before. "Sure."

"You'd better go down to the hotel and get a good sleep," she called after him. He did not answer. He trotted down the steps to the car, kicked it quickly into life and clattered off again into the beckoning prairie.

Chapter Fourteen

Homelessness is an art which develops with training. Mrs. Sondern and the children staked out their corner of Moose Jaw as adroitly and effortlessly as the nomadic Indians who had given the city its noble name. They walked quickly through the railway station, Mrs. Sondern bearing the wicker suitcase and the children carrying their winter coats and hats and wearing their overshoes with the buckles open, flapping along behind her like bright rag dolls blown by the slow spring wind. She looked up and down the wide street that ran along the railway tracks and led them directly toward a cluster of warehouses a dozen blocks away. They cut off into a back street behind the warehouses and there, as though by prearrangement, was the place they were looking for, a tiny hardware store with a second story above it and a sign outside that said: ROOMS. Within half an hour the first step of their resettlement had been accomplished with serenity and ease.

"Four dollars a week, lady."

"I couldn't possibly pay more than three-fifty."

"The last party paid four-fifty, but I always think it's worth something to have a nice family tenant."

Bea moved to the window. "My, what a nice view." The landlord glanced over her shoulder. Directly across the street another sign said: ROOMS, and two doors further down still another proclaimed: BEST ROOMS.

"Well——"

Beatrice had gone to the two open shelves of white china. "Of course I'd have to ask you to give me another cup and saucer and—oh yes, there doesn't seem to be a platter; I'd have to have some kind of a platter." Her hands rattled expertly in the shoe box full of cutlery. "And there doesn't seem to be any of the large spoons. I'd need three of those" —a slight hesitation—"say four in case of company." She smiled. "The children are so fond of soups and porridge."

"Well"—the landlord fought back his fury—"with a family tenant I don't mind making some kind of a—some people don't like children—but with me—I haven't any of my own, but——" He summoned back the remnants of his manhood and said sternly: "Three-fifty a week. Cash in advance."

"Of course," Bea said gently, opening her purse. The bed-sitting room contained two single beds, four chairs, a gas burner and sink, with bathroom privileges adjacent, and, quite unexpectedly and at first unnoticed, an ironing board, two extra quilts and half a tin of furniture polish.

After they had finished unpacking their clothes Mrs. Sondern gave Kally twenty-five cents to go to the nearest drugstore and buy a box of insect powder. "You just can't be too careful," she sighed. "This place is so lovely and clean and all it's almost sure to be a waste of money. But no matter how careful the proprietors are they can't always be sure about the people they let in. When we were living in Regina there was a man right next door to us who went to Toronto and stayed at one of the very biggest hotels there, they had the whitest sheets and towels you could imagine and a bathtub *and* a shower in the bathroom, and the very night he spent there there was some kind of a Kiwanis Club dinner in the dining room and a great big society dance in the ballroom, but he woke up absolutely covered with bites. It doesn't matter how nice a place is, you just can't be too careful. If there's any change left you could get some Life Savers, but be sure and save some for Harold."

She sent Harold to the newsstand for a paper. There were not many positions being advertised—only two in fact. One was for a cleaning lady at the Moose Jaw General Hospital, and the other was for a clerk, Grade III, in the government unemployment office. She and the children spent a pleasant five minutes talking about the clerking job and speculating on the pull and collusion that would be necessary for an unknown woman from Dobie to get it over all the Moose Jaw women with their ready-made connections. Then she put on her hat and coat and kissed them both good-by and went to the hospital, shouldered her way ahead of a haughty English lady in a far too stylish hat and a Norwegian lady with a far too belligerent jaw, and obtained the position as cleaning lady for five hours a day, six days a week, at thirty-five cents an hour.

She went home by the streets near the railway tracks, going back and forth along them, left and then along, then along the other street and then right, along for a block and then left. Then along and right, left and along, making a snakelike pattern parallel to the railway with all the turns right-angled ones. Three blocks from home she found what she was looking for, a grocery store of the most extreme decrepitude and meanness. The store's clapboard front had once been yellow, but the second layer of paint was entirely gone and the first layer clung to the graying wood only in occasional flakes and splotches. The white crescent of a Salada Tea sign on the store's one dingy four-paned window had lost fragments of all its porcelain letters and to a person unfamiliar with the meaning and periodicity of the original, it might have seemed to proclaim the whereabouts of some particularly disreputable and down-at-heels Greek fraternity:

SALADA

This, too, was one of the places that her private providence had prearranged for her. She walked in at once, and at the sound of the opening door a dark and timid little man darted to the greasy counter from the curtained doorway leading to the inevitable living quarters beyond.

He wore a soiled and very worn white apron above his collarless striped shirt. There was a gray stubble on his cheeks and something like an oriental glow behind his eager Balkan eyes. "Yes, lady?" he greeted her ardently.

Mrs. Sondern fingered her purse. The three dollars and seventy cents therein would have allowed her to pay cash for all she needed in this first transaction. But though she knew the next few minutes must bring pain to each of them, she also knew it would have harmed each of them—this ardent bobbing man as much as herself—to pay and be paid at once and to buy and sell and then part forever. Caused them both a temporary satisfaction but caused them both an irretrievable loss.

No, she had entered this store among all the stores because there was a reason to do so, because she had done a similar thing many times before and because there was nothing in it but good for everyone. She would not be weak.

"A pound of the bolony," she requested.

"Yes, missus," the grocer said gratefully. "You want it sliced?"

"No thanks," Mrs. Sondern replied, letting her eyes rove around the lean and dingy shelves of canned things.

The grocer cut a cylinder of meat from the longer cylinder inside his accordion-sized meat counter. He put it on his butcher's scales. "Pound and a quarter," he announced anxiously.

"That's perfectly all right," Beatrice said grandly. Now that she had listened a third time to the fearful-hopeful timbre of his voice she was certain that her judgment had been accurate. There was a heaviness about her heart for the eager little grocer, but it was tempered by the knowledge that he would come out of it well in the end.

"That bacon looks quite nice," she said. "I think I'll just have a pound of that too, now that I'm here."

His hands were trembling faintly as he wrapped the bacon. "Anything else? We got a special on beets."

"No beets," Mrs. Sondern replied decisively. "But I might take ten pounds of potatoes and a box of oatmeal and a dozen eggs."

The grocer moved less quickly now. Mrs. Sondern saw that he had begun to see. "And two loaves of that lovely looking pumpernickel."

"Yes, missus," he agreed miserably. He went back around the counter and began wrapping the bread in the *Times-Herald*. His bright eyes were not visible to Beatrice any longer; he kept them on his slowly busy hands, slowly busy wrapping the bread. "I guess you want credit," he said, like a dead man.

"I live near here," Bea replied, not too quickly. "I'll be dealing here all the time. I've just taken a position. At the General."

"Could you pay me something?" To the grocer it had now become as much a question of face as of anything.

"Fifty cents?" Bea asked hesitantly, making a concession she had not intended.

"I'll have to deliver it," the grocer muttered.

"Yes," Bea acquiesced sympathetically. This final nicety of their nicely calibrated understanding was so familiar to them both that it held embarrassment for neither. If he could not afford to insist on cash, neither could he afford to let her take the goods away until he was certain she had a fixed abode and where it was. "I'll be dealing here all the time, of course, and it will help us both if you know the way."

By the next day they were well and securely established. The children were enrolled at Victoria School, which was not far from their home. Beatrice had discovered a second-hand furniture store nearby, which, in return for the promise of an hour's scrubbing and cleaning a day for the next month, gave them a perfectly serviceable though disgustingly uncared-for davenport, a really quite solid little bridge table, and an absolutely huge framed copy of a painting by Turner. On the basis of the rapport thus established, the proprietor of the furniture store allowed her extremely favorable terms on the purchase of two dollars' worth of gingham curtain material, slightly faded to be sure, but almost certain to have been too bright in the beginning anyway.

On the third day Bea received her first wages from the hospital and made a payment to the grocer. He was so delighted that he made her take a pound of cocoa and a half pint of cream and half a pound of sugar—all still on credit—and as night drew in upon them in this large and so recently alien city Mrs. Sondern and her children found cause once more to sing a hymn.

Chapter Fifteen

Mrs. Chatsworth's attack came suddenly, only ten days after the departure of the Sonderns. When she had recovered sufficiently to arrange her thoughts, she was not so surprised about it as might have been expected. She had always understood that there was an element of heredity in these things and it had perhaps been inevitable that the source of Vanny's illness should disclose itself sooner or later, particularly since neither parent was growing any younger. For some months—perhaps years—she now felt free to confess to Dr. Harvison, she had had passing moments of dizziness. And she could remember having awakened on more than one occasion fighting for breath through a hard cartilaginous noose. But she had not troubled Bill with any of this and, of course, it would have been unthinkable to speak of it in front of poor Vanny.

Even as it was, Vanny hadn't been herself for a long time. Amelia had thought that the sudden departure of the Sondern family—so abrupt, so strange, she told Bertha Jessup; hardly waiting to say good-by; they *were* paid up though— would have restored their life to its calm and settled pattern.

So far as Bill was concerned, her expectations were fulfilled. The vaguely fidgety and restless air that had been growing on him ever since the strange family arrived was now altogether gone. He came home, ate his breakfast, sat reading for an hour, went to bed, got up and ate his supper, read some more and then walked back down to the station to begin his return run east. He said almost nothing and demanded almost nothing. They never mentioned his ridiculous escapade with the boy. But she was certain Bill was ashamed of his part in it now. Not that there was anything shameful in his motives. It was just that he had been so extreme, not just satisfied to help the boy out of trouble but determined to pretend the boy had never been in trouble, humiliating Billy Grier in public, humiliating the whole town in a sense, and certainly making a fool of himself and in the process conveying the impression that he valued the feelings of this juvenile delinquent above the feelings of his own wife and daughter. Wisely Amelia had communicated none of this to her husband in words and now that the visitors were gone he made his amends, sitting hour after hour in the warm kitchen with his books and magazines or rocking silently on the ivy-shaded porch.

But Vanny persisted in her disquieting attitudes and habits. The heart of it all was her absurd infatuation with that young man who played baseball. After one stormy scene on the night she had stayed out so late, Amelia had decided desperately that her daughter was passing through some difficult but transitory period of her life, like teething, and since Vanny had steadfastly refused to confide in her anyway, she had decided for the time being not to press the issue. She had no intention, ultimately, of failing in her duty as a mother, but there had never been anything like a test of wills between them before and it had come as an almost paralyzing shock to discover that Vanny was capable of taking part in one. When she had asked where Vanny had been so late and Vanny had kept repeating with the great stubbornness that comes only with great timidity, "I was detained," Amelia had been on the point of insisting that Vanny tell her the truth and tell her everything. She had been at first of a mind to make it clear to Vanny she must speak or make a hideous mockery of all the suffering they had endured together from the instant of Vanessa's birth. She had even framed the words and silently tested the tone of voice to go with them: "I can only think one thing, then. We're nothing to each other. We've never been." But she caught a trapped and frantic glint in Vanny's eye just in time, and bitter though the decision was, she decided for the first time in either of their lives that her daughter's reflexes were not wholly to be relied upon.

She never seriously entertained the thought that Vanny might have been bad or might be about to be bad. She had no real fear of losing Vanny to the baseball player; she had not been able to afford such a fear. But if no other thing was clear, it was perfectly clear that the baseball man was a menace to Vanny's health. Time after time Amelia had reminded her daughter, with the doctor's careful instructions as her own command, that she must not walk fast and must not allow herself to become excited. But sometimes Vanny almost ran down the front steps on the way to the library. Sometimes she came home with a flushed and hectic look. There was no doubt that the baseball player upset her, emotionally and physically, even though in the moral sense, with her character and her upbringing, she was far beyond any hurt he could do to her. And after that one long dismaying night, Vanny was never more than half an hour late coming home from the library. Amelia would have been a fool not to know that the baseball man was walking her to the corner and probably hanging around the library with her in the earlier part of the evenings. But patience had brought

Amelia so many of the things she held to be of value that she was not afraid to trust in patience again.

Nevertheless she had not expected the test to be so severe. Once the family upstairs went away and left them alone again, she had thought it nearly certain that Vanny would see of her own accord—or with only a little reminding—that Mr. Reiseling was an influence as superfluous and corroding to their own life together as the Sonderns had been. At first it had seemed that her instinct in this, given time, would prove to have been right. Vanny had been downtown doing the weekend shopping when the Sonderns departed. She arrived home only five minutes before the train was due to leave. Her first wild impulse had been to rush down to the station and bid them her own farewell, however fleeting, but in spite of the momentary state of agitation into which she had been thrown by the unexpected news, she had been persuaded that the exertion and excitement would be dangerous and of no real profit to anyone.

"Anyway, dear," Amelia soothed her, "I've already said good-by for you."

"But why did it have to be so sudden?" Vanny cried in perplexity. "I'm sure if they had had any intention, we'd have known. There was never anything secretive about any of them. They all seemed so eager to share things."

Amelia cut in quietly: "It's really none of our affair, Vanny. But I believe it had something to do with the excursion rates. Mr. Sondern apparently had finished what he had to do in Dobie a little bit sooner than he expected and they discovered that if they started out at once they could save a good deal on fares."

"Oh!" Vanny seemed half relieved to have an explanation and half disappointed that it was not more orthodox and definitive, like a sudden illness or a fire or a flood. She meditated uneasily for a few minutes and then followed her mother to the kitchen.

"Mother," she began timidly and unhappily, "there wasn't any—I mean, you and Mrs. Sondern——"

Her mother turned quickly and faced her. "You mean did I drive them away, Vanessa? Did I order them out of our home? Is that what you're asking?"

Vanessa was near to tears. Her mother drew her by the shoulder to the sitting room.

"Vanny," she said earnestly, when they were seated, "it happened exactly as I told you. But even if it hadn't happened that way it would have had to happen some other way. You see that, don't you?"

Vanny, dabbing at her eyes with a handkerchief, looked numbly at the floor.

"They weren't good for us. We weren't good for them." As Amelia leaned forward, a wisp of gray hair fluttered down across her cheek like some old and fading tendril of her very life reaching yearningly toward a renewal of understanding.

"Don't you see what's been happening to us ever since they came?" Amelia asked urgently. "We were so close together always, all the time. So loyal to each other, Vanny— so firm and loyal."

"But we still are."

"Not in the old way, dear. Not in anything like the old way." Amelia's desolate voice sank into silence. After a while she went on levelly: "Your father is the best of men, I'll never hear a word against him. But do you think in the old days—even a few months ago—he would have shown so little respect for you and me that he'd have gone and stood up in front of the whole community and said it was all right for that boy to steal, there must be no thought of punishing him? Do you think he'd have done that before?"

"But it—it was so kind."

"Kind? No, Vanny. Is it kind to teach a boy that he can steal and not pay for it, become a kind of hero for it? Is that kind?"

"But it would have hurt him so much more if they had punished him like that in public," Vanny said stubbornly.

"Perhaps," Amelia conceded mildly. "Perhaps." She paused and went on softly, "Perhaps if they had been ordinary people."

"What do you mean, Mother?" Vanny had put her handkerchief aside, her tearful dismay now leavened by interest.

"I hadn't meant to tell you this, Vanny, ever," her mother said slowly. "I still don't think it's good for your health to know these awful things. But better that than you should lose your sense of right and wrong. Anyway, everybody else knows it; you'd have found out sooner or later."

"What, Mother?"

"What do you know about Mr. Sondern? What was he doing at Dobie?"

"Why, he was the bank manager there and he decided to quit and take up farming. They were going to the Peace River Country to take a homestead if they could find one or buy a small farm if they couldn't. He's quit his job in the bank and he's going to join them there when he's finished winding up their affairs in Dobie."

"Mr. Sondern hasn't had a job for five years," Amelia said with gentle brutality. "He's hardly seen his family for five years. He's a common drunk. He's notorious all over the province as a drunk. He's a notorious drunk in Regina and Dobie and all up and down this line."

Vanny's sudden gasp told Amelia that she had broken it in the only possible way. None of this tolerance and those ridiculous "medical" explanations for drunkenness coming into fashion in the big cities and the big magazines had made any discernible impression on the pioneer standards of this corner of the province. The casual or accidental or capricious inebriate—say, like a good party man on election night or a growing farm boy celebrating sports day or a July the First dance—might be no more than an object of indulgent ridicule or sympathy. But a chronic drunk was an object of fear and loathing. Few people in these parts ever really got to see one, for, in spite of all civic legends, they were not rationed one to a village. There weren't that many to go around. But everyone had heard of the village drunk and held him in simple horror. If he had a wife and children, there was an amplitude of pity for them; but this too was tinged with horror; the natural horror of the whole and unsullied of the earth for the soiled and the misshapen. Vanny had half turned her back to her mother and drawn one knee up to the chesterfield. Her arm was thrown along the back of the chesterfield and she was weeping quietly into its crook.

"It's not for us to judge, Vanny," her mother reminded her compassionately. "But there's something else I might tell you. If Mrs. Sondern and the children hadn't left, he'd soon have been right here living with us right in this house."

Vanny turned and lifted her face again. "How do you know that, Mother?" She said it so quickly there was almost a hint of suspicion in it. "Did that have anything to do with their leaving? I thought it was the excursion rates."

"Oh, Vanny, Vanny," her mother murmured sorrowfully. "Why won't you trust me? Why do you make me tell you these terrible unpleasant things? Can't you see the truth, dear—they're running away from him. They can't help it. They must. There's nothing any of us could have done to prevent it."

"But how did you know he was coming here?" Vanny persisted.

"He—he telephoned. Only this morning. He—he as good as threatened to come. He was drunk then. He is drunk right now. Perhaps he's on his way here. That's why they had to go so suddenly, Vanny. Now aren't you sorry for wanting to blame me?"

Vanny had subsided, crushed and speechless, into the

crook of her arm again. Amelia's heart had never gone out to her daughter so much, even in the blackest days of her sickness. But she steeled herself now to do what she knew she had to do, for this was the moment in which it was best and most cleanly done. She crossed the room and sat on the chesterfield beside her daughter. She took Vanny by both shoulders and drew her around so that they were facing.

"Vanny," she said, "I don't want you to see Mr. Reiseling any more."

Vanny dropped her head and tried to pull away.

"You do see how bad it is?"

Vanny said nothing.

"Don't you, dear?"

"It's not anything like the same thing, Mother," Vanny whispered hesitantly at last.

"Not in all the details, but in the main things—yes." Her mother pressed Vanny's thin shoulders back so that it was a great effort for Vanny to avoid her suddenly bright exhorting eyes. "It's taking up with strangers. Wandering strangers, Vanny. Strangers who will come and go, whatever we want to do or whatever we can do. In and out of our lives, like snapping little beasts of prey. Tearing little shreds of us away with them, tearing away little bits of our happiness. Leaving us always like this, Vanny, all of us hurt and confused and a little bit smaller."

"It's not the same," Vanny repeated stubbornly.

"Have you done anything wrong with that man?" her mother asked her with an abrupt fierceness that took them both by surprise.

Vanny's drooping head shook slowly.

Her mother drew her close. "I knew you couldn't, of course." She stroked the girl's shoulder wordlessly. Then she said: "Vanny, until these last few months you had been getting so much better I'd been hoping—someday you'll be having your own home, Vanny. You'll be well and strong enough. But until that comes, don't let another wandering stranger spread more hurt and misery in the home we've all made together."

Vanny shuddered faintly but made no attempt to withdraw from her mother's arms. The two women sat in an oddly constrained embrace for several minutes. Then Amelia forced her daughter's eyes to meet her own again. She said firmly, "You won't see him again, will you, Vanny? Promise?"

Amelia thought, with a passing twinge of terror, that she saw some memory of the flicker of entrapment that had crossed her daughter's eyes the night she had confronted her on the porch. But it was gone in far less than a second.

"I promise," Vanny whispered.

It was by far the greatest shock of Amelia's life to discover that her daughter was not honoring her promise—even more horrible, had never, obviously, intended to honor it. She came home a little earlier from the library on the next three nights, but Amelia, peering from what had been the Sonderns' front room down through the Manitoba maples, clearly saw her part from the other figure at the corner. A greater sorrow still, she did not feel sure enough to confront Vanny with what she knew.

But there was, fortunately, still one place to turn. William, she knew, would have been no ally; he might, even, if the facts were laid before him, announce himself as an enemy in this matter.

But there was still one person to whom she could turn. Her friend, the doctor. Vanny's good friend too.

"Dr. Harvison," Amelia said with scant preamble, "I want to get Vanny away for a month or two. I feel she very much needs a change."

Dr. Harvison was afflicted with the most annoying of all the characteristics of a foolish man; there were times when ordinary tact demanded that he play the fool and these were the times when he saw fit to squander his tiny store of wisdom.

"Ah, yes"—he smiled wisely—"one of those afflictions that can't be cured by medicine. I've heard a rumor or two."

Amelia's lips grew firm. "The rumors," she said severely, "are unfounded. But it happens that having that rather buoyant family with us through so much of the winter and spring proved too stimulating for Vanessa. I'm sure you'd be the first to agree that she needs a lengthy period of relaxation."

"Well, now, let's look into that." Dr. Harvison was mildly hurt, but not so much so that he had any desire to offend the mother of his most interesting and senior patient. "As encouraging as Vanessa's progress has been to all of us, we all know she's still far from robust. Send her around for a checkup and I'm sure I'll be able to order her on a trip in the very best of conscience."

Mrs. Chatsworth did not look so pleased as he had hoped. She sounded almost impatient. "If it were just a matter of ordering Vanessa on a trip, I could do that myself," she said with a trace of asperity. "But it happens she is not anxious to go and unless she is anxious to go, or at least happy about going, I'm afraid the trip won't do her much good."

Dr. Harvison regarded her blankly. Amelia spoke again with a touch of impatience. "As a matter of fact, I've been feeling a little let down myself lately. I'm sure I need a rest and I'm sure if Vanny thought it were necessary she would not only be glad to go with me, but she'd insist on it."

Dr. Harvison reddened slightly. Then, adopting a somewhat more aloof and professional manner, he said: "Do you have half an hour to spare now, Mrs. Chatsworth? Good. Then, if we could just step inside?"

She had anticipated no difficulty with Bill and of course

there was none. The money wasn't important and, besides, he could get them railway passes to almost anywhere in the country.

Amelia had insisted that Dr. Harvison break the news to Vanny himself. Vanny had not seemed quite so alarmed as the doctor would have expected at first; she accepted his assurance that there was nothing to worry about rather more stoically than he would have thought likely. But of course she agreed at once to his suggestion that her mother would need companionship and that so far as that went she, Vanny, might profit from a little holiday as well.

The preparations for their departure went more slowly than Mrs. Chatsworth could have wished. Vanessa insisted that it would be quite out of the question for her to leave until she had had at least two whole weeks to help break in a substitute at the library. Then, perversely, she came so close to refusing flatly to buy her traveling suit at any of the local stores that it became a virtual necessity to order one from Eaton's catalogue, with a further slight delay.

Vanny insisted politely that her mother select their itinerary. Amelia sent away for a large batch of travel folders, but Vanny would only glance at them listlessly and say politely, "I'm sure I'd like any place you'd like, Mother."

Amelia tried in vain to stir her to enthusiasm. Vanny merely kept growing a little paler and a little more withdrawn each day and coming home a few minutes later each night from the library and pausing a few minutes longer at the corner.

"Banff?" her mother would say, hopefully. "It must be magnificent at this time of year."

"I've never been anywhere except in books," Vanny reminded Amelia courteously. "I'm sure any place you choose will be very exciting for me, Mother."

"I wonder if the Canadian National Exhibition would be too much for us?"

"Perhaps not a very good place for a rest," Vanny suggested with an equableness betokening a total lack of interest.

Amelia ranged as far as Cape Breton, Prince Edward Island, the Laurentians and Muskoka. Vanny said with implacable and mildly doleful sweetness that she was certain any one of them would be marvelous. It was not, Amelia realized with a great ache in her heart, that Vanny was being deliberately sullen. Her impending parting from the Reiseling man was a genuine sorrow to her, a dark and indefinite sorrow from which the poor girl could see no relief or release. If Amelia had been less certain of the rightness of her judgment, less certain of the rightness of living by the canons of order and continuity and fidelity, she would have been tempted to call the expedition off and hope against hope that Vanny would find her own means to the needed end right here at home. But her duty to Vanny and to William had no room for these dangerous indulgences. A definite date was settled for the trip and a definite deadline for deciding where they were to go.

It was on the day before this day for decision that Amelia had her attack. She was in the back yard hanging out the washing, and fencing, as she found herself compelled to do more and more often, with her meanly and maddeningly alert next-door neighbor, Bertha Jessup.

"I had the loveliest long talk with Vanny just now, just before she left to get the mail," Bertha Jessup said.

"Yes?" Amelia replied guardedly through a mouthful of clothespins.

"I worry about Vanny," Bertha Jessup said, with monstrous presumptuousness. "She looked so well there for a few weeks. But the last couple of weeks she hasn't seemed nearly as bright and cheerful."

Amelia disappeared soundlessly behind a flannelette sheet. But when she emerged again Bertha Jessup was still there.

"I think this trip will be a good thing for her. She says you still haven't been able to decide where you're going."

Amelia retreated furiously behind another sheet. When she came to the other side of the line, Bertha Jessup remained in a position of ambush. "Have you?"

"What?" Amelia asked shortly.

"Decided where you're going."

"It's not just my decision." Amelia managed, with a great effort of self-control, to keep her voice on a perfectly conversational level. "The trouble is that poor Vanny has never been anywhere at all before and she doesn't feel capable of offering a useful opinion. And I so much want her to enjoy it that I've been putting off deciding myself. But I guess that's what I'll have to do in the end."

She felt so pleased at having risen above this maddening woman on the other side of the fence that she now felt almost expansive. "It will probably be Banff."

"Could I tell you a secret?" Bertha Jessup asked. "You won't be angry?"

Amelia had a strong impulse to return to the other side of the row of laundry. But she looked up curiously.

"Vanny made me promise not to tell and I did promise. She just sort of blurted it out. But I've been thinking about it and, knowing the way you feel, I think it would be a shame if I didn't tell you anyway."

"Whatever are you getting at?" Amelia said, feeling the ferment of irritation again.

"Well, we were having this nice chat just now," Bertha Jessup said, "and I said to Vanny, 'But surely there's some place you're more curious to see than other places,' and Vanny said, 'Well, if there was only myself to consider and if it didn't mean dragging Mother all the way up there—— It's a funny thing,' Vanny said, 'I know it's not really so grand or even very comfortable, I guess it's just the sound of it, the way I've heard people talk about it.' 'What place?' I asked her again. For the minute she had the strangest look on her face and then she said, 'You know, Mrs. Jessup, someday I'd like to see the Peace River Country.'"

The words exploded across Amelia's mind in a white and shattering blaze. It was not a mere eruption of sound, but a collision of many sensations hammering wildly at the centers of all the senses. Between rushing waves of torchlit blindness she saw Bertha Jessup's thin clever mouth still moving and between swift cascades of deafness she heard Bertha Jessup's voice: "Hearing so much about it from those people upstairs and all—— Mrs. Chatsworth! Mrs. Chatsworth!"

The wandering strangers that come and go but never leave you, never go and leave you alone. Amelia lay on the grass of her back yard grappling as with a demon. But at last she was able to breathe again.

Vanny came home quickly. The doctor guided her gently into the bedroom. "There's every reason to hope," he whispered. He squeezed her arm encouragingly. "We already know the miracles that lie in care and sympathy, don't we?"

Vanny sank to the floor and clutched her mother's cold saffron-colored hand. The gray and desolate head on the pillow turned toward her.

"Vanny!" she whispered.

"Mother!" Vanny cried.

Amelia stirred and offered up a whimpered ejaculation of prayer. She could stand any suffering, now that the terror had passed away.

Chapter Sixteen

There come times to all people when, in certain of their endeavors, there is nothing left to do but accept defeat. A few have to accept defeat in everything. They are the ones who go lurching forward to their cruelly postponed conclusions with all the marks of acquiescence and even of approval.

"Yes," CPR Chatsworth said dutifully to the doctor, "we'll have to see that things are peaceful for her. She's worked hard. Now the least we can do is give her some rest and quiet."

"Yes," he agreed with Amelia, "he's not much, that Reiseling. He's not much at all. He's no good for Vanny. Not a bit good."

"Yes, Vanny," he said when she whispered a question to him once while Amelia was resting under the hypodermic. "Yes, there's no way anyone can stop you. You're of age. You can go away with him."

But then he was made to realize that he was contradicting himself. Contradicting things which had been ordained and against which he no longer felt disposed to struggle. He went on heavily: "You've got a right to go whether he marries you or not. You've got a right to hurt your mother. You've got a right to hurt yourself."

"Yes," CPR Chatsworth said to Dutch Reiseling, on a night when it was raining and the two of them were standing alone on the black wet veranda steps. "Yes," he said, "it would be hard on me to lose her. It would be harder on her mother. Her mother's under care twenty-four hours a day. But I can see your point." He thought for a long time, transfixing the solid-gold watch in his ponderous right hand with a painfully attentive stare. And then he said slowly, dragging out each agonized syllable: "You say you're only interested in discussing Vanny. All right. But you've got to remember—Vanny isn't well either."

"*Well!*" Dutch Reiseling shouted. "*Well!* God damn it! *Well!* If Vanny was any weller I'd go crazy. *Well? Well?* Mr. Chatsworth, you should know better. Touch Vanny's face. Touch her hair. Touch her arms. She's so well it drives me crazy and that's why I'm going to take her away."

"You've been drinking," Chatsworth interposed, staring ponderously at his watch.

"You're goddamn right I've been drinking!" Dutch Reiseling cried. "I don't always drink, but right now I'm drinking and I'm drinking good."

He put a firm but unexpectedly sympathetic arm on CPR Chatsworth's shoulder. "Look, Mr. Chatsworth. I don't think Mrs. Chatsworth is going to die. I don't think Vanny's going to die. You're not going to die and I'm not going to die. But let's say we're all going to die. There's still more good for all of us in me and Vanny living half an hour than all of us dying for a thousand years."

William Chatsworth heard a disturbed noise from Amelia's bedroom inside. "You'd better go," he commanded painfully.

"Don't worry," Dutch Reiseling said. "I'm not taking her

tonight. I'm taking her tomorrow. I'm buying a car tomorrow morning and we're going away."

Then Dutch Reiseling turned into the dark rain-drenched night and walked with surprising dignity almost to the sidewalk. Chatsworth watched him. Abruptly the ballplayer stopped, turned once, and came back to the veranda. He came quickly up the steps and touched CPR Chatsworth on the arm again, this time almost timidly. The older man peered through the soaked blackness; the jaunty and confident face of Dutch Reiseling now bore a puzzling intimation of uncertainty and want. "For Christ's sake," Dutch Reiseling whispered, "help us! If you won't help us, who will?"

And the next day Dutch did come back. Chatsworth did not know what he would do. He stood in the front room gently shaking his watch up and down in his palm. Amelia was in the back bedroom, resting. Vanny was sitting beside her, resting too and reading. The name of Dutch Reiseling had never been mentioned in the hearing of CPR Chatsworth and his daughter. It was a matter of knowledge and precedent to both of them that Vanny might sit there beside her mother until the end of all their allotted time and no one in that abode would come right out and say the name of Dutch Reiseling.

CPR Chatsworth looked up from his watch and through the window to the road outside where Dutch Reiseling had come back, as he said he would, and was now climbing out of a 1931 Ford coach.

Perhaps if Dutch hadn't had to stop a moment to fumble with the gate, the other man's decision would have been different. It took Dutch ten or fifteen seconds to master the rusty butterfly latch—long enough for a look of ancient misery to cross his face; long enough for him to dart a furtive embarrassed glance around him, long enough for Billy Chatsworth to know that even then the younger man wasn't at all sure what he would do next. Chatsworth's decision did not come to him full-blown in that instant, for he had been working on it doggedly all night. But it was now and now only that he knew which decision it was to be, now and now only that he knew beyond doubt that there was a saving streak of uncertainty, of plain human incompetence, in the strong young man who wished to take his girl away. Chatsworth stepped to the door and waved Reiseling back into the car. He made his wave slow and stealthy and the other man obeyed. Then he walked back into the house. He walked through the front room and into the bedroom. Amelia was lying gray and spent under a purple blanket. Vanny sat on a hard upright chair beside her, reading the woman's section of yesterday's Regina *Leader-Post*.

"All right," CPR Chatsworth said gently to his daughter. "All right. You have to go now, Vanny. You're twenty-two years old. And now it's time to go."

"Go?" Vanny questioned him softly.

"Yes." His voice was gruffer now, but he did not raise it. "Go away from home. All girls do sooner or later. You might as well do it now."

Amelia tore herself erect, clawing for support against the head of the bed.

"*Bill!*"

She looked at him in stunned and white disbelief.

"Bill! What in heaven's name are you saying?"

Vanessa had sunk to an impossible distance against the back of her upright chair. She regarded her mother for a moment and then stared in bleak helplessness at her father.

"Get up, Vanny," he commanded her gently.

"Get up," he repeated a little more sternly. "Get up and get ready to go away." He had only given his daughter one other direct command in all their lives and she had obeyed at once. He did not expect her to disobey now and he was sure, now that she fully understood him, that she would not disobey.

"*Bill!*" Amelia shrieked. She had sat up at first, but now she lay down with her head pressed hard against the pillow, and her arms pressed hard against her head. "In God's name, what does this mean?"

CPR Chatsworth reached into his inner pocket. "Here's some money," he said to Vanny. "There should be about sixty dollars. If you need more, wire me. From anywhere, any time. You don't have to be dependent on anybody—now or ever. But right now, Vanny, you can't live here."

Vanny had risen to her feet. "Mother!" she cried. "Mother!"

"*Bill!*" Amelia sobbed, raising and lowering herself with the help of the bedstead in steady convulsions. "*Bill!* What's this madness? Good God, Bill—what's this awful thing?"

"Get your things, Vanny. Get your things."

Vanny stood and tried to find a resting place for her blank and staggered gaze.

"Shut up, Amelia," CPR Chatsworth suggested gently. "Come on, Vanny."

He took her by the firm round arm Dutch Reiseling had spoken of so well—and he realized with sudden pleasure, so accurately—and he led her from the room. "She'll come back to say good-by after she's finished packing, Amelia. It won't be the last good-by. But right now I want her to go."

Dutch Reiseling was still there when they walked outside together, Chatsworth carrying Vanny's good brown suitcase and her mother's old black hatbox. Reiseling got out quickly to hold the door and Vanny got in quickly, not making any pretense that she was surprised to see him. Billy Chatsworth held his daughter's arm until the last. There were not many things he had seen in life. He had never seen the boulevards of Paris, or the lovely billows of the South Pacific, or the cool radiant tops of the Mountains of the Moon. But just as he helped his daughter Vanny into Dutch Reiseling's black 1931 Ford coach and just as he closed the door he did see this: he did see Dutch Reiseling's cool and splendid hand rest for a moment on Vanny Chatsworth's cool and splendid arm. And just before the door closed he did hear his daughter Vanny say something that would atone for many ancient disappointments. "God bless you, dear," she whispered to him. And Billy Chatsworth, who thought he had left God and blessing behind him, many years ago and through much attrition, touched his daughter's hand and whispered, "God bless you, Vanny, my dearest."

Then he walked back up the steps, opened the door, and went inside to rejoin and comfort his wife Amelia.

Chapter Seventeen

All along, Chris had considered his plan without flaw. It had come to him, not through conscious thought but in a startling burst of interior light, at the very moment when he had begun to fear that thought might not produce a solution.

His own arrival in Moose Jaw had been delayed by almost a week. Forty miles out of Elevator he had run Roxy Brannick's Chevrolet across a shallow ditch and head on into a telephone pole, leaving the car in a state of almost complete ruin and himself in particular need of another drink. In the next town he found a man who was willing to buy what was left of the car for a hundred and ten dollars, cash and no questions asked, and another man who was willing to supply him with drinks up to a reasonable limit.

He still had sixty dollars left when he got off the train in Moose Jaw. He stood in the waiting room of the station, studying a calendar, realizing for the first time how many days he had lost and trying to strike some kind of an equation between the money left in his pocket and the days left in which to pursue his quest. So long as he had money, he

was prudent enough to recognize, he would have a reasonable amount of leisure in which to conduct his search, but
if he ran out of money before the search was fulfilled, the
search might become secondary.

He estimated he was good for almost two weeks, allowing,
say, seventy-five cents a day for food, four dollars for rye,
and another dollar for an occasional beer or quart of loganberry wine. It was not a reassuring thought. He did not dare
enlist the aid of the police or other official agencies; he considered it doubtful that Roxy would have reported the loss
of the Chevrolet, but there was no way of being sure, and if
he got mixed up with the police, he might never find them.

He stepped out of the waiting room onto Manitoba Street
and glanced tentatively up Main Street. "Don't worry,
Bea," he muttered, "I'll find you. I won't let you down." But
the flat city, hugged close to the ground and full of the movement of a beginning day, looked much bigger than it was and
he felt no real confidence at all.

It was in that moment that the plan had come to him.
The schools! Bea had always been a great one for education.
Even if they were only intending to stay here for a few
weeks, she would be sure to have the children at school by
now. All he had to do was to go around to the schools, sys-
tematically and one by one, and wait until he saw the children. He would walk up to them and say: "Hello, Harold.
Hello, Kally," and they would take him by the hand and
lead him home.

It was a perfect plan, and he had not begun to doubt it
until the eighth school. At the second school he had perceived that there were certain elements of difficulty, even
within the plan. Standing a block away from the second
school, watching the children trooping toward its meshed-
steel gates, he had seen a boy and a girl walking together on
the other side of the street, not fifty feet away, and he had
been certain that it was those he sought. "Kally! Harold!"

he shouted happily, and stumbled into the roadway, holding out his arms to them. The children stopped in their tracks and looked at him with open mouths. Then they turned and fled from him, with impossible, sobbing swiftness.

He stopped running toward the children and went back downtown, chiding himself for his foolishness. He had assumed he would know them instinctively the instant he saw them, but he now perceived there was nothing to support this easy theory. Except for the brief, opaque, barely remembered glimpse of their faces on the day of his arrival in Dobie, he had seen neither of them for almost four years. Children grew, they changed. Unless he was very careful, very systematic, he might see them and not know them at all. He sat in a beer parlor all one evening, working out their ages and projecting his memory of a seven-year-old Harold and a six-year-old Kally into a future that was really the present and letting his mind dwell, with loving exactitude, on the imagined face of an eleven-year-old Harold and a ten-year-old Kathleen. It was not really so hard a thing to do, once you approached it with a plan. Kally looked so much like her mother and Harold so much like his father that the only thing he had to do was to pretend it was a dozen years ago, and he and Bea were miraculously united, untouched by the intervening sorrows. It had to work, it simply couldn't fail. "How many public schools in Moose Jaw?" he asked a stranger sitting at a nearby table in the beer parlor. "I don't know," the stranger said, and asked another stranger. Soon there was a large solemn discussion about it, with several other strangers joining in, and Chris obtained not only the number of schools, which was ten, but a smudged and much amended list of their names and approximate locations.

But now, a week later, he was working on the eighth school and he still had not obtained success. He took great pride in the way he had worked up to now, with as much orderly zeal as though he were back in the employ of the bank. Each night he was in bed not later than midnight in the tiny room he had taken in a tiny hotel near the railroad tracks. He sat in the beer parlor, pacing himself, until closing time and then went to his room, carefully measured out a half tumbler full of rye in a water glass and sipped slowly at the rye while he washed out a shirt in the washbasin beside the bed. He had spent six dollars of his capital to buy two new shirts; it took a shirt two days to dry, and by washing one every night and running his hands over the wrinkles before he hung it up, he was able to ensure that when he set out in the morning he was always clean and presentable. He shaved himself each night just before going to bed.

He was always at the school by eight-thirty, in plenty of time to see even the earliest arrivals. He usually walked up and down on the opposite side of the street, pausing every now and then to inspect the numbers on the houses, as though he were charged with delivering a message to a strange address. In that way he could keep a careful watch on the gate into the schoolyard, and if he saw a boy or a girl approaching the gate at whom it seemed well to look more closely, he could hurry across the road and ask for directions to a certain street. Not that he considered this innocent subterfuge absolutely necessary; but he was so accustomed to being asked for explanations that the mere avoidance of explanations had become an end in itself.

He was inspecting a house number a block away from the eighth school when a boy and a girl approached the gate together. To see them accurately he had to look into the morning sun, and even then their faces were not wholly clear. He hurried across the street and intercepted them with a polite shout. "Excuse me, please." The children stopped. As Chris drew nearer he saw that there was not the slightest resemblance to the children he was looking for. "I don't suppose there's a little girl in your class named Kathleen, is there?" he asked politely. "They call her Kally for short."

"No, there isn't, mister," the girl said.

"Well, thanks," Chris said. He was about to turn away. Neither the boy nor the girl had moved. They were both staring over Chris's shoulder toward a point two or three hundred yards down the street. Chris turned in the direction of their eyes. A fat policeman was marching quickly toward them, his head thrust forward a little on his bulky neck, as though he were drawing a bead on a target.

"Well, thanks," Chris said again, and started to saunter back across the street.

"You stay right there!" the policeman shouted, and began to run.

Chris began to run too. At first the movement was involuntary, entirely primitive, but as his thin legs gathered speed, it entered his mind that he was running not merely for the sake of running, not merely because the policeman was running after him. Roxy had told them. Roxy must have told them about the car, after all, told them how to trace him through the woman in Elevator. Ah, Roxy, if you only knew what you've done to me. His sudden dread lifted his thin body like a gust of wind. He darted around a corner, down a back alley and out onto a busy street. A bus was just pulling away from the corner and he stepped aboard.

He spent the rest of the morning in his hotel room, writing a letter to Roxy Brannick.

Dear Roxy:

What a friend I turned out to be! I guess you think I'm lower than a snake's behind and I guess you're right.

But Roxy, I still need your help. I've got to have it, Roxy. I know I haven't any right to ask for anything from you, especially after everything you did for me before and the way I paid you back. But I've got to have your help again, just this one more time.

He looked at what he had written and sighed deeply. Ah,

Roxy, it's the literal honest-to-God truth I'm telling you. He poured himself a drink of rye and surveyed the page with a swelling heart.

I know you told the police about the car. You had a right to do that, anybody would have done the same thing. They nearly caught me today. They know I'm in Moose Jaw. Maybe they'll catch me tomorrow. They'll catch me sooner or later, Roxy, unless you write to them and tell them it was a mistake. Tell them somebody else took the car, Roxy, tell them you've found it. Tell them they've got no reason to look for me.

I'm not asking this just for myself, Roxy. If it was just myself, I'd take what's coming to me and not complain. It's my wife and kids I'm asking you to think about, Roxy.

He stopped and let his mind play sadly on the misunderstanding that had come between him and his friend, between him and his good and final friend.

The reason I left like I did was that Bea phoned me that morning. The boy was in trouble and she begged me to come. I had to go, Roxy. But I couldn't tell you, could I, because I'd already told you that whatever happened or whatever I said you had to stop me from going.

Well, now I've found them, Roxy. We're together again and everything is perfect. You'll never believe this, Roxy, I wouldn't have believed it myself, but I'm right off the sauce. Maybe one or two drinks a day, never any more. I seem to have lost my taste for it. I don't give a damn whether I have it or not.

He stopped again. This is true, Roxy; it's true because it will be true.

I'll tell you everything, Roxy, so you'll know I'm not trying to hide anything. I've put my address up at the top of the page. We're going to Grande Prairie, Alberta. We always intended to go there, away back before we were married. Maybe if we'd done it then things would have turned out different. We'll get a farm, farms are cheap up there. I'll pay you back for the car, that's the very first thing I'll do. And then maybe you'll think better of me, Roxy. Maybe you'll come up and visit us. There'll always be a drink waiting, even if I won't guarantee to join you every time. I've finally had to admit I can't handle it.

He closed his eyes and threw the bridle off his mind and turned it loose to roam in the soft pastures of the future. Ah, Roxy. Ah, Bea. There never was a man as lucky as me.

So, Roxy, you can see what it would mean if there was any trouble over the car. I haven't got the car anyway, Roxy. I bust it to smithereens on a telephone pole. Please, Roxy, think it over and do just one more favor for

Your No-Good Friend
Chris Sondern

He remained close to the hotel for three days, judging it would take that long for Roxy to withdraw the charge concerning the car. He slipped out and bought himself a secondhand tweed jacket and a brown fedora hat. Whatever happened about Roxy and the car, he still had to go to the last two schools.

Roxy Brannick read the letter again and sat frowning heavily over the answer.

Dear Chris:

I didn't call no cops. If anybody's bothering you it must be about something else. You could have taken the car, the tractor, the combine and the Percheron stud and I still wouldn't call the cops.

I'm not mad at you, Chris. If things don't work out,

you come on back here. If you get in trouble you wire or phone me.

Your Also No-Good Friend,

Roxy

P.S. You aren't off the sauce no more than a rabbit. I'm hoisting one to you right now. The next one you have, you hoist it to me.

Roxy folded a twenty-dollar bill inside the ruled sheet of paper and put it in an envelope.

Chapter Eighteen

Milk, two thirds quart. Porridge, half box. Bread, loaf and half. Butter, nil. Sugar, half pound. Cocoa, quarter pound. Eggs, four. Bacon, two strips.

Mrs. Sondern thrust a hopeful hand into the far corner of the upper cupboard. Her fingers closed around the cool curve of an unsuspected bottle and she gave a tiny start of pleasure. She drew what she had found into the morning light and smiled in rueful recognition: pickles, two.

Her felt slippers went tut-shush tut-shush on the worn linoleum floor as she carried the bread and the peanut butter to the kitchen table. She listened briefly for the steady breathing of the children on the other side of the curtain she had improvised from the two spare blankets and a length of cord across one end of the room. She decided they were still sleeping soundly and that it was safe to raise the raddled green blind concealing the back yard.

She went back to the table and cut eight thick slices of bread. She began spreading them with peanut butter. She cut the slices extra thick because just this one day the children would have to go without milk for their lunch. Not that it would hurt them: if they were any healthier she'd have to call a doctor. There was no problem about breakfast because there was enough porridge and plenty over for two other meals.

The troubles of affluence. She chuckled at the sudden, raffish thought. She was now working seven hours a day at the hospital instead of five. Her pay was now forty cents an hour instead of thirty-five cents. It came to sixteen dollars and eighty cents a week; so much more than they could possibly need that it had for the time thrown all her calculations into a state of chaos.

She had been given her first ten dollars and forty cents only four days ago. In her eager haste to put everything on an orderly and businesslike basis, she had somehow become too ambitious. She had paid Mr. Mikayous four dollars and eighty cents in cash all at once. She had bought Kally a new skirt and she had bought Harold two new pairs of socks. They had all gone to see Wheeler and Wolsey in *Rio Rita*, and had had strawberry ice-cream sodas afterward. Then, just before they went to bed, Harold had had one of his worst fits of despondency. One minute they were all laughing together over the memory of Wheeler and Wolsey and waiting for the milk to boil for their good-night cup of cocoa and the next minute Harold was shouting blackly: "We'll never get there, will we? We'll never get there at all!"

Bea was not hurt by his outburst. On the contrary she was touched by it, touched by the thought that he had kept it so valiantly suppressed in the far worse times they had just passed through. Touched by and even a little proud of the incorruptible streak that would not permit him to forget the larger need in exchange for the smaller indulgence. Proud that he had had the courage to be brave in adversity. Proud that he had had the courage to be afraid in good fortune.

Harold had always needed so much reassuring. There was

so much difference between them. If there had only been Kathleen—Kathleen who was so much more pugnacious and hard to bruise—it might not even have been necessary to set a goal at all. But Harold needed things to look toward. Things grand enough to stir him in spite of himself but not so grand as to seem beyond his reach.

"But, Harold," Beatrice whispered, "we will!"

"No, we won't." He did not sound superior or martyred, just solemnly resigned. "No, we won't."

"You make me sick!" Kally stood up and shouted at him across the table. "Just because we had a little fun—you had as much fun as anybody—now you're trying to say we're wasting all our money. Peace River Country, poof! If that's the way you're going to act, I say that as far as the Peace Riv——"

"That will do, Kally!" For the first time in years Beatrice felt as though she might be about to cry in front of the children. She could not tell which stood more desperately in need of reassurance: Harold, denying their faith, or Kathleen denying the need of faith. She herself still needed no reassurance at all and it took her only a moment to recover her calm.

"Now, look here, both of you!" she said sternly. "Harold's right. Tonight was just a little spree. There won't be many more. We've got to save up. Now sit down and finish your cocoa."

She went to the clothes cupboard and dragged out the wicker suitcase. She rummaged around in its furthest corner and produced a piggy bank that Harold's father had once given him. It had been used only briefly for its intended purpose. Its two pristine pennies still rattled around in it, six years after they had been put there.

Mrs. Sondern put the bank on the lower shelf of the cupboard. She opened her purse. She emptied the contents of the purse on the table. There were three one-dollar bills and sixty cents in change. She took one of the bills and folded it lengthwise down the middle. Then she folded it again and doubled it. She walked to the cupboard and shoved the bill through the slot in the china animal's back.

"One." She did the same thing with another bill. "Two." And then with a third. "Three."

She addressed the children in her most persuasive tones. "Every week we're going to do that. No matter what happens we'll put three dollars in the bank every week. No matter what we do, no matter what we have to have. That's the Fund. When we have enough for the fare to Calgary, we'll go to Calgary. Then we'll start another fund there. And then we'll go to the end."

"See?" Kally taunted Harold.

"Well——"

It was a good plan, Beatrice told herself again, as she went on with the children's lunch. Perhaps she had allowed her sense of order to go a bit too far. But her frown soon vanished as she recalled a piece of information she had stored away a few days earlier. If you were on the regular staff, there was a janitor on night shift who would loan you up to four dollars a week; at the end of the week you paid back his four dollars with only another dollar for his trouble.

She looked out the window and saw there was a touch of frost on the ground. The children might as well have an egg for breakfast as well as the porridge; they wouldn't be having milk for lunch just this one day.

She walked back around the draped blanket that passed for a curtain and touched Kally on the shoulder. The girl sprang up in the bed like a Jack-in-the-box in red and yellow flannel.

"Hi!" Kally giggled. "I dreamed I was a white horse."

Mrs. Sondern kissed her, walked over to the davenport, and stroked Harold's disheveled head. Harold opened one eye slowly, closed it, opened the other and closed it too. And then he opened them both at once. "I heard her," he complained. "I bet she didn't dream that at all. I bet she made it up."

"And later I was a lion," Kally went on implacably. "A huge golden lion."

"Like fun!" Harold objected.

"Now, now," Beatrice admonished.

"Harold dreams about being a midget," Kally goaded him. "Once he dreamed he was a hunchback; another time he dreamed he was a snail. There's no use saying it isn't true, Harold, because you told me so yourself."

Harold's voice shook with outrage. "That was only once! I dream all kinds of things."

"Kathleen!" Mrs. Sondern said sharply. The children fell into a forced and bargained silence.

Mrs. Sondern went back and wrapped the sandwiches in the classified pages of yesterday's newspaper. She studied the date. They had been here thirteen days now. She hadn't really been afraid that Chris would find them; if there had ever been a reason for such a fear it was gone now. Chris either got things done quickly, while the impulse was on him, or he never got them done at all. She wondered whether he had really even reached Elevator, whether he'd even left Dobie. Probably not. If he had, and if he'd had the energy to keep going, he'd have guessed that Moose Jaw would be their first stop. Moose Jaw was a divisional point, and he must have known they couldn't possibly have saved enough money to go further. But whatever he'd said to Mrs. Chatsworth, Chris had probably realized how wasteful and cruel it would have been to try to find them here.

There were many things to be regretted. One of the things she regretted most in this moment was that so few people realized that side of him: he was a very intelligent man and a very considerate man. There were a thousand instances she could give, but beside his one tiny but catastrophic flaw it was hard to make anyone believe in their importance. A thousand thousand instances. Now she was being foolish again and there was nothing to be gained from foolishness. She closed her eyes and put her hands on the table and gave silent notice to the prayer she had offered every night and every morning since their parting. "Please, God, make my husband well and bring him back to me. Make our children's father well and bring him back to them."

Then she dismissed Chris from her mind and went to the stove and served the children their porridge.

Just before they left for school she remembered something. "Oh, by the way, I picked up a *Times-Herald* in one of the wards yesterday. There's something I want to read to you. Here: 'City police today reported that a dark thin man has been accosting children near the city's public schools almost daily during the last week or more. So far no child has been molested, but Moose Jaw parents are urged to warn their children not to talk to strangers. Special patrolmen have been assigned to watch school areas.'"

She had already made up her mind not to read them the last paragraph. "Although there is no positive evidence, police fear the man who has been loitering near the local school-yards may have some connection with the brutal slaying last Tuesday in Regina of nine-year-old Mary Hudson."

"Ha!" Kally cried in excitement. "A burglar! A highwayman! Ha! Just let him try!"

"Huh!" Harold muttered back at Kally. "Look who's talking!"

"Ha!" Kally repeated. "A brigand. A footpad. A confidence man. What's a confidence man, Mother?"

"Never you mind," Bea said, reaching over to smooth Kally's hair. "Just pay attention."

"I'll turn into a golden lion. I'll turn into a white horse. I'll eat him alive. I'll kick him to death."

"Aw, come on," Harold said impatiently. "Let's get going."

Chapter Nineteen

Chris was more guarded now, but more determined. He could not afford to wait forever, but before he chose the next school he bought a street map and studied it with some care. He decided Victoria was the safer of the two still left to visit. It was away across the town, kitty-corner from King George, and if the police were still looking for the man who had stolen Roxy Brannick's car, it seemed likely that they would not be looking there. He had resolved that he must appear even more businesslike and purposeful. He had bought a tie to go with his jacket and as he inspected himself in the mirror he assured himself with some confidence that he didn't have a thing to worry about. Sooner or later he might have to go back to King George, but it seemed much more likely that they would be living close to Victoria. The houses there were much less splendid than the houses around King George; it was an older, less expensive district and the moment he walked past the school for the first time he began chiding himself for not having gone to Victoria before going to any of the others.

He walked briskly past the gate along High Street almost

as far as Main, then crossed the road determinedly and walked past again on the other side. It was still early. Fewer than half a dozen children were playing in the schoolyard and the street was almost deserted.

A black car drove slowly up High Street. Chris crossed the street again. The car made a U turn and came back toward him. When it reached a point directly opposite him, it came to a sudden stop. Both the back doors flew open and two men in gray business suits jumped out into the street. "That's him!" Chris heard a voice cry.

And then he was running again, incredibly running faster than the men in the gray suits, who did not have the advantage of running for all that was left of their stake in the universe. He ran past a picket fence of gaping faces, some of which fell away from him in wide-eyed fright, some of which shouted oaths and warnings to the faces ahead. Occasionally a pair of arms reached out from the environs of a face and tried to interrupt his flight. He beat them off with savage fury. He ran on into Main Street and across the intersection of River, with a tiny wake of stunned silence always just behind him and then a little further behind a mounting tumult of fretful cries and loud vengeful footsteps. He ran across Manitoba and into the big dim railway depot. Halfway across the waiting room his own panting and the awful slap-slap-slap of his thin shoes on the stone floor were the only sounds in the tall dark cavern. But then the noises of pursuit spilled in behind him, lashing and threatening.

He stumbled down a dim inclined corridor, pushed a uniformed guard out of the way and ran up a stairway. He burst forth on the station platform, blinded momentarily by the harsh sunlight. The narrow aisle of concrete on which he stood was sealed in on each side by a standing line of passenger cars. He dived under the nearest and scrabbled across a bar of cinders. A line of boxcars awaited him on the other side. He dived under the closest car before he realized it was moving. He threw the top part of his body back with a weary, sullen hopeless heave, and as the wheel passed across his knees he cried out as much in apology as in protest.

And now there entered his life an unending series of miracles, unbelievably beneficent, unbelievably illogical. There was no call for any of it. The men in the gray suits were upon him almost the instant that it happened, tearing off their gray suits to dam up the first murderous deluge of his blood and then tearing off their clean silky ties, while he lay and watched, and twisting them quickly around the thin mangled stumps of his legs.

The gods showered him with gifts, a lifetime of gifts, fantastic beyond all the riches of Cathay. They got him to the hospital still fully conscious, still reasonably strong and alert, and there they presented to him a very sensible young doctor and a very knowing young nurse.

"I'm going to die," Chris whispered to the sensible young doctor and the knowing young nurse.

They did not, of course, agree formally that this was to be the case. They prepared blood for him and prepared needles for him, just as though he was going to live, but when he told them his name and told them that his wife was somewhere in this strange town and that he must see her, they did not cling to the illusions sacred to their calling. They did not insist on going through all the stainless, sanctified rites of an art they knew now to be useless.

"Don't put me to sleep," Chris pleaded. "Don't let me go to sleep."

"I think there's a woman named Sondern on the caretaking staff," the knowing young nurse said. "It's a very unusual name."

"We won't let you go to sleep," the sensible young doctor said gravely to Chris.

And in a while, a very short while, Bea came into the room and lay down on the bed beside him. He was still able to see her face, rather dimly as though through a bad and smudgy pane of glass, but that made it, if anything, better. All the irrelevancies were erased from her face; it rested on the pillow beside him like a tranquil cameo of the girl in the Athens Café in Regina.

They did not talk. They had never found it essential to talk, and they did not talk now. They lay quietly in each other's arms, husbanding the time left to them. There was ample time. Time to think not only of the Athens Café but of Wapella, Sask., and Shaunavon, Sask. Time to think of Al Ritchie and Leggy Firbank and the ballroom on Portage Avenue.

"Royal Alex," Chris murmured once.

"Yes, dear," Bea whispered back.

Nothing more was said. Chris found a bare spot on one of her arms and he caressed it with his fingers, rejoicing in the tiny movement of flesh against flesh until he fell asleep.

It was late in the day, toward the close of afternoon, when the children were taken in to see him. They had been sitting, deathly still, in a small room outside the ward since a little after noon, not caring to talk about the sparsely solemn details which had been brought to their attention, one detail at a time and with no hint of their final meaning. Kally had tried once: "Imagine Daddy being in Moose Jaw all this time and us not knowing about it!" And they had both perceived the hopelessness of encompassing so much all at once and had ceased trying. They sat there politely drinking the cocoa and eating the sandwiches that the nurses brought them and talking about baseball and storybooks with the interns and probationers who knew what they were doing there and kept coming in and out of the room with no other apparent purpose than to pretend they didn't know. Two or three times their mother came and sat with them for a while and then went away again when a nurse opened the door to the nearby ward and beckoned to her.

At last, late in the afternoon, their mother came and said quietly: "You can see your father now."

Kally rose quickly and took her mother's hand. Harold licked his lips nervously and tried to think of an excuse. "Are you sure it's all right?" he whispered piteously. "I mean, is it all right? I don't mind waiting."

"It's all right, Harold," his mother said, and Harold stole into the room a step behind the others. Kally went over to the bed at once. Her shoulders were shaking and Harold could see them shaking and he knew they shook from some emotion far more awful than mere grief. But she went over to the bed and she put her head down close to where the white hand wavered up at her from the white bedspread and took the hand in one of hers and held it close against her cheek. She remained there for several minutes and in that while Harold brought himself to look at his father. To his surprise he could detect no suffering on the dark face on the pillow. He could not tell what else might be there, for the light was fading, but as his eyes ran down the weirdly flat surface of the coverlet, his mind held an image of the violated helpless creature imprisoned below and the pity he had begun to feel was lost in a wallow of horror. There was no limit or focus for his horror; it embraced all men and all ventures, all circumstances and all involvements.

"Come here, son." The soft voice from the bed, so helpless and so full of yearning, folded in on his pounding heart and enclosed it in a tight envelope of fright. He looked quickly toward Kally and then toward his mother, half expecting to see a signal for flight. Kally's eyes were squinched up almost shut and although it was too dark for him to see the tears wobbling along their rims, he recognized the look for her crying look and knew the tears must be there. Their mother's gaze, reaching imploringly for his own, was full of desperate encouragement.

"Come closer, son."

They can't make me. I can't do it and they can't make me. Come closer is the trouble. It's behind all the trouble, now and ever. Further is what we need. It's the only thing that's any good to us. Closer is a trick, it's always been a trick for people like us. Closer might be good for other people, for people who live in big houses and aren't always going away on dark trains from small houses that they don't own, and getting run over by trains, and getting caught stealing, and having stones thrown at them, and doing other people's washing, and making things that nobody wants to buy, and——

"I hope you're feeling better, sir."

Harold had never called anyone "sir" before, not even a school principal. But certain boys in certain books that he had read had called their fathers "sir"; it seemed to be the ultimate pledge of solicitude and respect and the words stumbled forth now unpremeditated and uncontrolled. In this moment of dissolution and forced abandonment he was feeling very sorry for all of them, the other three quite as deeply as for himself.

"Harold?" His father had raised his head anxiously from the pillow, a hard-fought inch or two, and his voice was louder than it had been yet, almost a cry.

"Yes." Harold still had not moved.

"Remember when you were little and we used to do the magic? Remember the magic we used to do?"

"Yes," Harold whispered.

"I think my coat's in that cupboard over there. There should be a pack of cards in there in the coat pocket. I always carry a pack of cards. I still do them every time I get a chance."

Harold, puzzled, remained silent.

"Get them, Bea," his father whispered weakly. "Get the cards, please."

"You're too tired," Harold blurted, now not far from panic. "We'd better not, Mother. We'd better go and let him get some rest."

But their mother was already back at the bed with the cards. She eased Mr. Sondern's head up a few more inches and then tucked the second pillow under his head and placed the cards in his white hands above the white bedspread, level with his chest.

"I always promised I'd show you how," Harold's father said slowly. "And now I'm going to show you." His fingers caressed the red backs of the cards for a few moments and then he held them weakly out, across the edge of the bed.

"Take a card," he whispered, "any card."

A note of fanatical urgency carried the words to him and Harold crossed the room in the furrow they had left in its anxious silence, as powerless as water following a rivulet downhill.

"It's all in the way you've got the cards stacked," his father whispered. "Start with the ace of clubs, then the two of diamonds, three of hearts . . . and so on through the deck. Take a card."

Harold reached out quickly, drew his hand back and looked down into the cup of his palm. Eight of diamonds. The picture of the eight of diamonds usurped the last corner of his thoughts; for the moment it had crowded out even his awful desire to escape.

His father whispered: "Then you sneak a look at the next card after the one they take." Harold ceased staring at the eight of diamonds. His father's head jerked upward with a start, and his father cried out in alarm: "It's too dark in here! Turn on the light, Bea!"

Their mother reached across and switched on the cylindrical head lamp. In the sallow, antiseptic bath of light, everything lay still and frozen, their father's face clenched with determination, his black eyes glowing like a terrified kitten's, one white hand clenched around the thick rectangle of cards held face down on his chest. *It's hurting him,* Harold suddenly knew, *it's hurting him so much he can hardly stand it.* And with this came the first realization that his father was about to die, and the first intimation of something else, something almost as big as the fact of death. It was an intimation only, not a complete understanding; a swift, half-seen vision of the grandeur of defeats endured but not admitted; a glimpse into the splendor of gifts that are given without shame for their smallness, given in pride because that is all there is to give.

"I've got a card," he called gently. His father did not stir. "I've got a card, Dad," Harold called to his father again. He brought the eight of diamonds up to the level of his face and through a soft rush of tears it swam and undulated like a torn red flower floating down a river.

His father's head strained forward on the pillow and with feeble stealth his white hand raised the other cards an inch above the white bedspread. "Six of clubs," his father whispered.

"That's right," Harold whispered back in triumph and wonder. He opened his fingers and let the eight of diamonds swim out of sight to the floor. "You got it, Dad. There's not many people can do that trick," he whispered proudly.

His father's head had fallen back on the pillow. The lines of strain eased a little on his faded face, and when he closed his eyes they were more at peace.

Chapter Twenty

Spring came earlier here. The country was still quite flat and nearly bare. Nothing broke the prairie except an occasional poplar bluff, naked to the sunrise, the slender trellised branches of its trees a web of gold filigree against the blood-shot sky. But the graying patches of snow were much thinner than they had been the day before. When the train took a curve, Mrs. Sondern saw a faint suggestion of the foothills far ahead.

She reached across the double seat of the day coach and touched the children's shoulders in turn, massaging them quietly to wakefulness.

"Soon be there," she said.

"Where?" Harold asked, suddenly and unnaturally wide awake. "Where?"

"Calgary, silly. Remember? Come on, Kally."

Kally yawned with luxurious diffidence. "Who cares," she complained, snuggling into the corner by the window.

"Come on, now. Come on, Kally."

"Oh, all right." Kally squirmed to her feet, shaking herself resentfully. "I've been dreaming."

"What about, dear?"

"About the Christmas cards." She set her face in careful retrospect. "Whoo!" she giggled. "*What* I dreamed!"

"What, dear?"

"We sold eighty-five dozen. The very first day."

"Eighty-five dozen!" Mrs. Sondern laughed giddily. "Eighty-five dozen. My goodness, the Acme people would faint if we sent them an order for eighty-five dozen."

"Well, that's how many it was," Kally insisted. "Whoo!"

"Whoo! is right. Do you know how much that would be in commissions? Over sixty dollars. Over a hundred if they bought the three-dollar line."

"They all bought the three-dollar line," Kally said.

"Well," Mrs. Sondern said staunchly, "it's real good value at that." She fumbled with the wicker suitcase and brought out a small fiberboard album. Kally came across the space between the seats and sat beside her while she leafed through the pages, pausing to examine the glossy samples.

"This is my favorite." Mrs. Sondern sighed. "X-29. I always liked the old English scenes."

"I like the one of the Virgin."

"B-12," Mrs. Sondern said. "It's very nice too."

"What's your favorite, Harold?" Kally asked.

"Aw, I don't know."

"But you must have a favorite," Kally protested.

"Aw, I like them all."

"You certainly sound as if you do," Kally said indignantly.

"Well, I still think it's too early to sell Christmas cards," Harold answered sulkily. "How can you sell Christmas cards in April?"

"That's just the thing," Mrs. Sondern said. "That's where you've got the jump. You've got the whole field to yourself."

"And there's the extra commissions too," Kally reminded him severely.

"Yes, Harold, there's the extra commissions to consider

too. The Acme people, they're very alert progressive people, they give a 20-per-cent bonus for all orders received before September."

"There's nearly seventy thousand people in Calgary," Kally added.

"I know," Harold said in a more conciliatory tone. "I wasn't trying to start an argument."

Mrs. Sondern replaced the album fondly in the suitcase. The train had crept unnoticed through a series of crevices in a plateau of oil tanks and warehouses and now it had quietly ceased to move. "My goodness," Mrs. Sondern said. "We're here."

On the way through the gate into the depot she said: "I think I'll just ask the Traveller's Aid about a place to stay. They're usually very good."

"Let's go and see about the fare first," Kally said. "Just so we'll know."

"Yes," Harold said eagerly. "Let's do that first, Mother."

"All right," Mrs. Sondern said. They walked across the rotunda of the waiting room together and the children pressed close in behind as Mrs. Sondern stepped up to a vacant wicket.

"I wonder if you could give me some information about fares to the Peace River Country," Mrs. Sondern asked.

"Certainly," the man behind the wicket replied. "I'll just get the Northern Alberta schedule." In a while he came back. "It's quite a long way," he said apologetically, as he thumbed over the timetable. "It's a lot further from here than most people think. Just a minute now."

They stood close together beside the wicket, waiting.